CATHERINE MANN

HIS EXPECTANT EX

Silhouette Desire

Published by Silhouette Books

America's Publisher of Contemporary Romance

W9-BRR-619

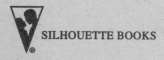 SILHOUETTE BOOKS

ISBN-13: 978-0-373-76895-0
ISBN-10:   0-373-76895-8

HIS EXPECTANT EX

Visit Silhouette Books at www.eHarlequin.com

Printed in U.S.A.

Recent books by Catherine Mann

Silhouette Desire

Baby, I'm Yours #1721
Under the Millionaire's Influence #1787
The Executive's Surprise Baby #1837
†*Rich Man's Fake Fiancée* #1878
†*His Expectant Ex* #1895

Silhouette Romantic Suspense

*Private Maneuvers #1226
*Strategic Engagement #1257
*Joint Forces #1293
*Explosive Alliance #1346
*The Captive's Return #1388
*Awaken to Danger #1401
*Fully Engaged #1440
Holiday Heroes #1487
  "Christmas at His Command"
*Out of Uniform #1501

*Wingmen Warriors
†The Landis Brothers

CATHERINE MANN

RITA® Award-winner Catherine Mann resides on a sunny Florida beach with her military flyboy husband and their four children. Although after nine moves in twenty years, she hasn't given away her winter gear! With more than a million books in print in fifteen countries, she has also celebrated five RITA® finals, three Maggie Award of Excellence finals and a Bookseller's Best win. A former theater school director and university teacher, she graduated with a master's degree in theater from UNC-Greensboro and a bachelor's degree in fine arts from the College of Charleston. Catherine enjoys hearing from readers and chatting on her message board—thanks to the wonders of the wireless Internet that allows her to cyber-network with her laptop by the water! To learn more about her work, visit her Web site at www.CatherineMann.com or reach her by snail mail at P.O. Box 6065, Navarre, FL 32566.

To my parents, Brice and Sandra Woods, a beautiful testament of enduring happily-ever-after at over forty-five years of marriage and still going strong!

One

Sebastian Landis had been in courthouses more times than any hardened criminal. He was one of South Carolina's most successful lawyers, after all. But today he'd landed a front-row seat for how it felt to have attorneys hold complete power over *his* life.

He didn't like it one damn bit.

Of course getting divorced ranked dead last on his "things I like to do" list. He just wanted to plow through all the paperwork and litigation so the judge could make it official.

Gathering files off the table in one of the courthouse conference rooms, he barely registered his goodbyes to his attorney and polite handshakes with Marianna's counsel. Power ahead. Eyes on the finish line. Clipping his BlackBerry to his belt again, he kept his eyes off his wife, the only woman who'd ever been able to rattle his cool—his calm under fire being a renowned trait of his around courthouse circles.

At least they'd completed the bulk of the paperwork with their lawyers on this overcast summer day, leaving only the final court date. The settlement was fair, no easy feat given his family's fortune and her thriving interior decorating career. They hadn't even fought over the dissolution of their multimillion dollar assets—probably the first time they hadn't argued.

The only wrinkle had come in deciding what to do with their two dogs. Neither wanted to lose Buddy and Holly, or split the sibling pups up. Ultimately, though, they had each taken one of the Boston terrier/pug/mystery parent mutts they'd rescued from the shelter.

What would they have done if he and Marianna actually had children?

He backed the hell away from that open wound fast. Not going there today, no way, no how, because even a brief detour down that path kicked a hole in his restraint on one helluva crap day.

Which left him checking on Marianna in spite of his better judgment.

She rose from the leather chair, too damn beautiful for her own good, but then she always had been. With dark eyes and even darker long hair, she'd been every guy's exotic fantasy when they'd met on a graduation cruise to the Caribbean.

Thinking about that sex-slicked summer would only pitch him into a world of distraction. Scooping up his briefcase, he put his mind on what he could accomplish back at his office with the remainder of the afternoon. Of course he could also work into the evening. It wasn't like he had anything to go home to now, living in a suite at his family's compound. He reached the exit right in step with Marianna.

He held the door open, her Chanel perfume tempting his nose. Yeah, he knew a lot about his soon-to-be ex, like what scents she chose. Her favorite morning-after foods. Her preferred lingerie labels. He knew everything.

Except how to make her happy.

"Thank you, Sebastian." She didn't even meet his gaze, her lightweight suit skirt barely brushing against him as she strode past and away.

That was it? Just a thank-you?

Apparently he could still feel something besides attraction for her after all, because right now he was ticked off. He didn't expect they would celebrate with a champagne dinner, but for heaven's sake, they should at least be able to exchange a civil farewell. Not that civility had ever been one of his volatile wife's strong points. She'd never been one to run from a potentially contentious moment.

So why was she making tracks to the elevator, her designer pumps clicking a sprinter's pace? God, she made heels look good with her mile-long legs. She'd always been a shoe hound, not that he'd minded since she modeled her purchases for him.

Naked.

Damn it all, how long would it take for the flashes of life with Marianna to leave his head? He wanted his polite goodbye. He needed to end on a composed note, needed to end this marriage. Period.

Sebastian made it to the elevator just before it slid closed. He hammered both hands against the part in the doors until they rebounded open. Marianna's eyes went wide for an instant and he thought, oh yeah, now she'll snap back. Toss a few heated words around and maybe even the leather portfolio she gripped against her chest.

Then boom. Her gaze shot straight down and away, looking anywhere but at him.

He tucked into place beside her, the two of them alone in the elevator chiming down floors. "How's Buddy?"

"Fine." Her clipped answer interrupted the canned music for a whole second.

"Holly chewed up the grip on Matthew's nine iron yesterday."

His brother had pushed him to play eighteen

holes of golf and unwind. Sebastian had won. He always won. But unwinding didn't make it anywhere on the scorecard. "Luckily, Matthew's in a good mood these days with his new fiancée and the senatorial race. So Holly's safe from his wrath for now."

She didn't even seem to be listening. Strange. Because while she'd stopped loving him, she still loved those dogs.

He normally wasn't one for confrontation outside the courtroom, but he'd seen enough divorce cases to know if they didn't settle this now, they were only delaying a mammoth blow up later. "You can't expect we'll never talk to each other again. Aside from having the final court date to deal with, Hilton Head is a relatively small community. We're going to run into each other."

She chewed her full bottom lip, and just that fast he could all but feel that same mouth working over his body until he broke into a sweat.

He thumbed away a bead of perspiration popping on his brow, irritation spiking higher than her do-me-honey heels. "Seems we should have spelled out the rules for communication in that agreement. Let me make sure I get the gist of this right. We aren't speaking anymore except for hello and goodbye. But is a nod okay if we're both walking the dogs on the beach? Or should we section off areas so we don't cross paths?"

Her fingers tightened around her leather portfolio, her gaze glued to the elevator numbers. "Don't pick a fight with me, Sebastian. Not today."

What the hell?

He never picked fights. She did. *He* was the calm one, at least on the outside. So what was going on with her? Or with him, for that matter? "Was there something with the lawyers that didn't go the way you hoped?"

She chuckled, dark and low, a sad echo of the uninhibited laughter that used to roll freely from her. She sagged back against the brass rail. "Nobody wins, Sebastian. Isn't that what you always say about divorce cases?"

She had him there.

Sebastian planted a hand beside her head. Sure he was crowding her but they only had one more floor left for him to get his answer. "What do you want?"

Marianna raised her eyes, finally. That dusky dark gaze sucker punched him with the last thing he expected to find, especially after they'd spent six months sleeping apart. And he saw the one thing he absolutely could not resist taking when it came to this woman. Marianna's eyes smoked with flaming hot…

Desire.

Her marriage began and ended in the backseat of a car.

Marianna had eloped with Sebastian Landis at

eighteen. They hadn't made it to a hotel before hormones got the better of them, and they pulled off on a side road. Now, after the final appointment with their lawyers, hormones—and emotions— once again blindsided her.

And all because of a fleeting moment of regret in his eyes when they put it in writing about splitting up Buddy and Holly. That hint of vulnerability from her stoic-to-a-fault husband had turned her inside out.

Then turned her on.

She'd tried to haul buggy out of the conference room before she did something stupid, like jump him. No such luck. They'd barely cleared the elevator with their clothes on before sprinting through the rain to his car. He'd peeled rubber out of the lot and pulled off at the nearest side road for isolated parking.

Frantic to ease the ache between her legs if not the one in her heart, Marianna hooked her arms around Sebastian's broad shoulders as he angled her over the reclined seat and into the back. The tinted windows offered additional privacy in their wooded hideaway. Spanish moss trailed from the marshy trees like sooty bridal veils, at once both beautiful and sad.

Raindrops pounded the roof in time with her blood gushing through her veins. Lips locked, she tumbled and twisted until they settled into the lengthy backseat, Sebastian's Beemer roomier than the Mustang convertible he'd driven as a teen.

They also didn't have an unplanned pregnancy confining their moves this time.

Sebastian looped his tie around her neck and tugged her toward him. Melting into the familiar feel of him, Marianna inhaled the spicy scent of his Armani aftershave, rich with whispers of how often she'd inhaled the same smell as it rode the steam of his morning shower. Greedy with the need to take all she could this one last time, hungry after months without his body, she explored Sebastian's mouth with her tongue as fully as her hands roved his shoulders, back, taut butt in pin-striped pants.

"Marianna, if you want to stop, say so now." A damp strand of brown hair fell over his brow in a downright blaring statement of rioting emotions from a man reputed to be the most ruthless litigator in the state of South Carolina.

"Don't talk, please." They would only start fighting. About his interminable hours at the law office. About her temper as flamboyant as some of the homes she decorated.

About how they had absolutely nothing in common except physical attraction and the precious babies they'd lost.

Thunder growled and he cupped her face in his hands, electric-blue eyes snapping sparks through her, echoing the snap of lightning overhead. "I need to hear you say it, that you want me inside you as damn much as I want to be there." His low growl spoke of his own strained control. "We have enough regrets without adding one more to the pile."

"I only know this is a heartbreaking day and I have to have *this*." She couldn't bring herself to say she wanted him, not after all the times she'd needed even just his presence only to spend another solitary evening on their balcony with only the rolling surf, a top-shelf wine and her salty tears. "Now, can we put our mouths to better use?"

He kept his gaze firmly on her face while his hand slid down, his thumb brushing a distracting back and forth along the side of her breast. "We can end the conversation, but that won't stop me from telling you just how sexy you are."

His eyelids lowered to a heated half-mast as he dipped his head to nip at the oh-so-sensitive curve of her neck. Knowing every button to push to send her writhing against him, achy, needing. More. Now.

"Or how much you turn me inside out with the way your legs look in those heels. Yellow. God, who wears yellow shoes?" His broad palm slipped under the hem of her skirt, up the length of her thigh in a hot path as he traced the edge of her panties right between...

Her head fell back as words scrambled together in her overheated mind. "Me. I do. And they're lemon-colored."

"They're hot."

If only great sex and a whopping big bank balance were enough, they could have made it to their golden anniversary, no problem. That thought could douse the pleasure brought by his talented fingers faster than emptying a silver ice bucket in their laps.

She tore at the buttons on his monogrammed shirt, popping, opening, scraping back fine fabric until her palms met warm skin. The flex of hard muscles contracting beneath her touch blocked out the world waiting beyond the abandoned forest nook. She kissed, nipped, laved over him while Sebastian tunneled his hands through her hair until it slipped free of the loose twist, tumbling midway down her back.

His BlackBerry buzzed an unwelcome interruption. Her skin started to chill. He tore the handheld off his belt and tossed it to the floor impatiently.

About damn time he did that.

Marianna gripped his shoulders, fingernails digging half-moons into his flesh as she strained to get nearer, desperate to deepen the closeness. Twining her fingers in his close shorn hair, she held his face to hers, devouring him, ravenous after the months of going without.

Sebastian nudged her jacket aside, down her shoulders, and cupped her breast through the satin camisole. He circled a thumb around the tightened crest sending sparks of want through her. When he lowered his mouth to replace his hand, she couldn't control the urge to roll her hips against his.

"Enough." The moist heat of his mouth as he worked the satin over her skin tightened the swirls of pleasure. "More."

And thank goodness he understood the contradiction of impulses that had plagued most every part of their marriage. He angled them both upright again until he sat in the middle of the seat. Marianna straddled his lap, her suit skirt hitching up as she knelt, her toes pressing against the front seats until her Gucci pumps began to slip off.

His hands reached down, gripping both shoes and holding them in place. "Leave them on," he growled low, "I'm suddenly a big fan of lemon."

She fumbled with his belt, just above the hard press of his desire straining against his zipper. Then yes, she found the enclosed velvet length of him, stroking. Never one to lag behind, Sebastian slid his hand beneath her skirt again, fingers twisting in the thin string of her thong, pulling the panties lightly biting into her flesh. She welcomed the pinch on her over-heightened senses and then it...

Snapped.

He pitched aside the insubstantial scrap of yellow silk she'd worn to make her feel like more of a woman and less of a failure at the most important relationship of her life. Marianna positioned herself over him, and he thrust upward. Fast. Hard. No fumbling. No awkwardness. Rather a synchronicity gained from nine years of knowing just how to come together with sex if nothing else.

She grabbed his wrists and moved his hands to cup her breasts. Her fingers stayed with his over her while he pounded into her with an urgency as powerful as the storm outside and the man inside. Marianna rocked her hips against him in grinding circles, milking every ounce of sensation from this last explosive encounter.

One last time to be together.

One more memory to tuck away and torment herself with over a glass of wine by the beach.

If only they could communicate half as perfectly on anything as well as they connected during sex. Even that bond became strained because of the looming "after" time, a free-fall into sadness because there was nothing else left between them.

Sweat slicked his chest, her arms, their kisses turning slightly salty in her mouth. Pleasure built and clawed inside her, the need to finish almost painful. His hands twisted in her hair, his jaw tight in a way she recognized as Sebastian waiting for her, holding back until even his arms shook. Her moans mixed with his, urgent, faster. Exploding through her in a release that satisfied even as it destroyed another corner of her weary soul.

Pleasure rippled over the pain in a bittersweet farewell mix. Wave after wave surged and receded until she sagged against him, his arms still banded around her as his body rocked with aftershocks.

The confines of the Beemer echoed with only their panting breaths and the tapping rain. Marianna knew they had nothing left to talk about. It was over between them. They just had one last meeting before a judge in a few weeks.

It wasn't like they even needed to discuss their lack of birth control. Her miscarriage nine years ago had left her infertile. Not that they hadn't continued to try—and fail.

Then hope had briefly returned. Sebastian had been a hundred percent on board with adoption, and for four blessed months Marianna had been a mother. Little Sophie's face stayed as firmly planted in her memory as in her heart. She and Sebastian had put aside their marital problems bubbling to the surface and poured themselves into parenthood.

Only to have Sophie's birth mother change her mind.

Lying against Sebastian's chest this last time, Marianna ached to cry, for herself, for him, for their daughter. But when a person dried up inside, tears were tough to find. Six months ago, Sophie had been plucked from her arms, their home, their lives.

Marianna's heart broke. Sebastian went to work. And their marriage finally fell apart.

Two

Hilton Head Island, South Carolina—
Present day:

Marianna winced as the judge raised his gavel and—*whap*—cemented everything she and Sebastian had spelled out with their lawyers in the divorce paperwork.

In the span of one day, she'd become both a divorcée and an unwed mother. A baby. She gripped the edge of her chair to keep from flattening her hands to her stomach.

After so many failed attempts at conception, miraculously one of Sebastian's swimmers had managed to circumnavigate all her cysts and scar tissue. She'd only found out this morning—an axis-tilting moment that still left her reeling.

A tiny flutter of hope stirred like the life she looked forward to feeling move inside her. Just maybe this time...

She had considered telling Sebastian before court—for all of five nauseating seconds. This didn't change anything about them as a couple. Custody paperwork would be a separate matter altogether. Besides, she wanted to be a hundred percent certain with a doctor's visit. She wasn't going on the voucher of one pink plus sign, not after nine years of disappointments, after the past months of hell from losing Sophie.

And how would Sebastian feel about the news?

He loomed a few feet away—how could the man loom even when he sat?—thumbing closed the locks on his briefcase. Scowling. At least something was normal in this upside-down day.

She gathered her resolve and crossed the aisle. "Sebastian, I would like to set up a time for us to talk. Perhaps someday next week?"

After she'd visited an ob-gyn. She'd missed the signs at first because of her heavy workload decorating two major Hilton Head homes, then assumed the stress of the impending divorce had thrown off her cycle—even when one missed period became two.... It had been two months since she'd ditched her panties in the backseat with Sebastian.

Standing, he smoothed his silk tie and refastened a button on his suit jacket. "We can talk now. Let's wrap everything up at once."

"I can't today." She had an urgent appointment with a pack of crackers and a flat surface.

"Something more pressing to do?"

"You're the one who's married to his Black-Berry." Bile burned the back of her throat. "I wanted to give you enough notice to wedge three minutes with me in between appointments, court and catching up on your e-mail."

"Nice." His tight smile didn't even come close to reaching his eyes.

But true. And sad. "I'm sorry. I didn't intend to rehash old ground." She pressed her palm to her forehead to ease the swimming dots of frustration swirling in front of her eyes. "This isn't a good time to discuss anything, which is why I want to meet with you next week. I'll call your secretary and set up an appointment."

She spun away on her heels, only just managing not to fall on her face. She grabbed the end of a row for balance until the floor stopped wobbling underneath her.

Sebastian braced a hand on the small of her back. "Slow down and take a deep breath. It's only natural you're still upset from the proceedings."

"Upset? *Upset!*" Glancing over her shoulder at

him, she swallowed a bubble of hysterical laughter. She wanted to cry and pitch plates and rail at the unfairness of her greatest dream being tempered by such a total crap day. "As always you're the master of understatement."

He pinched the bridge of his nose for two of those steadying breaths before looking at her again, his expression a little too close to pity for her liking. Ire kicked up a storm in her already churning stomach.

Sebastian slid his hand from her back to her arm for a tiny squeeze as he stepped closer. "So now you want some kind of goodbye-over-coffee moment."

Her body reacted through instinct to the familiar heat of him, the scent of his aftershave, the strength of his touch. How long would it take for time to dull the sensory memory of just how good he could make her feel?

She plucked his hand off and aside. "We said our goodbyes in the backseat of your car." Anger, hurt and fear all left her itchy and irritable. "Your conjugal rights officially ended about five minutes ago."

He would no doubt have plenty of opportunities to indulge himself with all the starry-eyed students that floated in and out of his successful practice. She'd seen a virtual entourage of admiring females in his law library some nights when she'd come by to pick him up late.

"Okay, okay, take it easy." He backed her into

the privacy of a quiet corner. He flattened a hand on the wall beside her head, his body creating a barricade between her and the onlookers staring at them with ill-disguised interest. "I completely understand that future shoe fashion shows have been canceled."

Marianna scrunched her toes in her silver Jimmy Choo slingbacks and willed down the memories that would only wound her. Heaven knew that when she hurt she let it out with anger. But she would not cause a scene.

It was hard enough getting through these past few hours while her mind taunted her with images of what the day could have been like. If only she'd been able to surprise Sebastian at the office with a mug that read "Real Men Do Diapers" or some other cute coded announcement.

Of course he probably would have been in court or taking a deposition.

Oops, there went her temper again. *Breathe. Breathe. Breathe.* "It's not about a civilized cup of coffee. There are just some, uh, loose ends we need to discuss when we're both calmer. I'll talk to you next week, somewhere neutral and public."

He held his position, almost touching, his gaze assessing her like some witness on the stand for endless seconds.

His BlackBerry buzzed. He ignored it. But still...

"You had that on during our divorce hearing?"

She backed away, all hopes of calm long gone. "We definitely shouldn't talk today."

"Fine, whatever you want."

It wasn't what she wanted by a long shot, but there wasn't any other choice. "Goodbye, Sebastian."

But it wasn't really farewell and she knew it. There would be no clean break for them now. Marianna ducked under his arm and toward the exit. She had one week to shore up her resolve and make plans.

She double-timed down the hall, barely registering that his big wonderful family sat on benches waiting. Just the kind of oversize clan she'd dreamed about as a lonely only child of elderly parents, who'd loved her, yes, but now even they were gone.

She pressed her hand to her stomach, her silver bracelets clinking, and prayed all the harder for the tiny life inside her. Her heart pounded faster. Or wait. Those were footsteps approaching her— Sebastian's, of course. He wasn't letting her off that easily. How strange that while he never fought, he always won.

Sebastian punched the elevator button for her, cocking his head to the side as he studied her with his piercing litigator stare. Oh God, she so didn't want to climb into that claustrophobic box along with resurrected visions of their last ride.

"Uh, thanks, Sebastian, but I think I'll take the stairs."

She turned too fast and the world grew tighter like a narrowing focus of a lens. Her knees gave way, and all she could see on her way down were Sebastian's Ferragamo loafers she'd given him last Christmas.

"We should call EMS," Sebastian's stepfather said for the third time, his voice booming with all the authority one would expect from a three-star general.

Sebastian agreed. But the doctor—at the courthouse to testify in a hearing—seemed to think seven minutes and forty-one seconds of unconsciousness wasn't anything to worry about yet. Dr. Cohen sat on the edge of the sofa, the young professional reading her watch while holding Marianna's wrist in her hand.

After Marianna had landed at Sebastian's feet in a fall as fast as his own stomach, he'd scooped her up and made tracks for an adjacent conference room. He'd stretched her out on a sofa, slipped off her shoes, loosened her pink jacket, while his mother hovered and the General located help in the form of Dr. Cohen.

While he'd asked his family not to come to the courthouse, they'd shown up anyway. It was a good thing after all.

Two of his brothers clumped in a corner with his mom and the General. Standing. Waiting. Sebastian hated inaction, a big part of why he enjoyed his job.

There was always something to do, some way to charge ahead and take control.

Why wasn't Marianna opening her eyes? And how many times would that doc count a pulse? Duke medical credentials be damned—and yeah, he'd asked when she started checking Marianna over. Dr. Cohen would just have to live with being overridden if his ex-wife didn't wake up in the next ten seconds.

Sebastian knelt on one knee beside the sofa, lifting Marianna's other hand, too cool and limp in his grip. "I'm going to take her to the E.R. now. If she wakes up on the way, great. And if she doesn't—" What could be wrong with her? "She'll be at the hospital all the sooner."

The doctor stood, pulling her glasses off to hang from the gold chain around her neck. "That's your call to make, of course, as her husband."

Husband? Now wasn't that a kick in the legal briefs? But he didn't intend to correct the doctor and lose what tenuous ground he held over Marianna's medical care at the moment. He shot a quick "mouths shut" look over his shoulder to his wide-eyed family.

A low moan from Marianna yanked his attention back to the sofa. Her lashes fluttered and he squeezed her hand.

"Marianna? Come on, wake up. You're scaring us here."

"Sebastian?" She elbowed up to look around,

massaging two fingers against her temple. She blinked fast, her gaze skipping around the small room filled with nothing more than a conference table, swivel chairs, the sofa and concerned relatives. "What happened?"

"You passed out in the hall. Don't you remember?" If any day was worth forgetting, this would be it.

She sagged back, her pink suit skirt hitching up her legs. "Oh, right, the courthouse, your Ferragamo shoes."

He didn't know what the hell his shoes had to do with anything, but at least she grasped the gist of the day.

His mother nudged him aside and placed a damp handkerchief over Marianna's forehead. "Here, dear, just lie back until you catch your breath."

"Thank you, Ginger." Marianna accepted the cool cloth with a grateful smile.

Why hadn't he thought to do that? "How are you feeling now?"

She looked away, apparently more interested in the window blinds than in seeing him. "I forgot to eat breakfast. That must have sent my blood sugar out of whack."

"What about lunch?" He pointed to the industrial clock over the door. "It's three o'clock."

"Already?" She peeled the damp cloth from her forehead and dabbed it along her neck. "My nerves must have gotten the best of me. I couldn't bring myself to choke anything down."

If Marianna couldn't eat, something was seriously wrong. This woman loved her food, one of the things he'd enjoyed most about her. Watching her savor oysters on the half shell had landed them in bed more than once. "Have you been sick?"

She sat upright, swinging her feet to the floor beside her silver slingbacks. "Thank you for your concern, but I'm responsible for myself now that we're divorced."

Dr. Cohen's eyebrows rose. "He's your *ex*-husband?"

Marianna nodded, glancing at the clock. "As of about a half hour ago."

The physician brought her red-rimmed glasses to her mouth and nipped lightly on the tip. "Taking that into consideration with a low blood sugar level, no wonder you fainted." She gave Marianna's wrist a final pat. "And here I was assuming you must be pregnant just because that's my specialty."

Marianna winced and looked away as she'd done countless times over the years when people mentioned babies. The purple stains of exhaustion below her eyes broadcast the additional stress she'd been under lately if anyone looked beyond a credible makeup job. Sebastian stepped between her and the doctor, territorial, protective.

Shaking loose of that husband appellation and all the urges that came with it was easier said than done. "That's not what's going on, but we will find the real reason for her fainting spell."

How many times in the past had he diverted conversations from the seeming unending litany of well-meaning and sometimes downright intrusive comments?

When are you going to make me a grandmother? Isn't it time to start your family?

You and Marianna treat those dogs like children. I guess not everyone wants babies.

Dr. Cohen backed away, scooping her bag off the conference table. "My apologies for jumping to conclusions. Of course there are plenty of other reasons for fainting besides not eating. If the problems persist, however, I do recommend that you check in with your regular physician." Hitching her bag over her shoulder, Dr. Cohen paused at the door. "Now if you'll excuse me, it's probably about time for my turn in the witness stand."

The General escorted the doctor out with a thank-you while Ginger hovered just off to the side. "Marianna, dear, we're glad you're all right. Please know that you can call on us if you need anything."

Like prideful, strong-willed Marianna would ever show that kind of vulnerability. He was still shocked as hell she'd asked to meet with him next week.

With soft spoken goodbyes, his family cleared out, leaving him alone with Marianna for the first time since they'd torn each others' clothes off in the back of his car two months prior.

Damn, silence sure did weigh a lot.

He leaned back against the conference table, his arms crossed over his chest to keep from touching her. "I don't think you should drive yourself home."

She slipped her slingbacks onto her feet, drawing his attention to slender long legs. "And I don't think it's wise for us to get in your car together again."

"Still want me that much, do you?" he couldn't resist retorting.

"Don't be an ass." Her eyes snapped with barely restrained anger and something else he couldn't quite define. "All I want is a nap."

He needed to focus on her health, not those creamy legs that wrapped so perfectly around his waist. "You should see your doctor or go to an E.R. if he's busy."

"I have an appointment for the end of the week. I called this morning."

His legal eagle instincts piqued, urging him to dissect her statement. "If you're feeling that ill, why wait until the end of the week?"

Silently, she stared back, blinking quickly, her chest rising and falling faster by the second. He'd spent the last three years since passing the bar exam interrogating witnesses, and he had a good knack for spotting when a person was hiding something. And he knew without question, Marianna had a secret lodged somewhere inside that beautiful head of hers.

He intended to discover that secret before they left this room.

Three

"So Marianna? Why wait four days to see the doctor if you can't eat and you're passing out?"

Marianna stared back at her narrow-eyed ex and experienced a total empathic bond with butterflies pinned to a display board. Somehow Sebastian knew she had a secret, and he wasn't setting her free until she ponied up information.

Did the state bar pass out internal lie detectors when awarding licenses? She had two choices here. She could brush him aside and wait for the doctor's verdict that Friday. If she wasn't pregnant, she wouldn't need to say anything to Sebastian.

Except she knew in her heart, against all the

odds, somehow she carried his baby, which brought her to the other option. Tell him the truth now, because if she didn't he would be royally pissed next week.

And rightfully so.

"About that time a couple of months ago, in your car when we, uh…"

"Right, I remember." Heat stirred in his eyes.

Of course he did, but hearing him admit it rekindled the steam of their raw goodbye. She could almost smell the rain and sex in the air. "We didn't use birth control."

His eyebrows pinched together. "Of course we didn't. You're not on anything, and I don't carry any with me because we…" his voice slowed as his forehead smoothed "…don't need it."

She stayed silent.

He shook his head, opened his mouth and shook his head again. "You're pregnant?"

She nodded, shrugging, still not able to form the words after so many years coming to grips with the idea of *never* having the chance.

He sunk into a leather conference chair, his face completely expressionless in spite of the slight paling. "You're pregnant."

"I'm fairly certain I'm two months along."

He scrubbed a hand over his jaw. "I already figured out the two months part."

"Thank you for not asking whose it is." She couldn't have taken the pain of such an accusation on a day when her emotions were already stripped bare.

"I guess I'm not the total ass you seem to think I am."

"You've questioned my hours at work often enough."

He'd quizzed her about time with her boss more than once. Sure Ross Ward had a playboy reputation, but damn it, Sebastian should have known she could be trusted. She'd been hurt by his unfounded suspicions. He vowed he could read the truth in people's eyes, but he'd sure missed the boat on that one with her.

He folded his arms over his chest, the swivel chair squeaking back. "Are you trying to start a fight by bringing up Ross Ward?"

"Of course not. There's no point. With DNA tests, it's easy enough to prove paternity these days."

Sebastian stood and paced away, resting his palms on the window ledge. His broad shoulders stretched the dark suit jacket as they rose and fell heavily. "We're having a child."

It still seemed surreal to her, too. "If all goes well."

He pivoted hard and fast toward her. "Is something wrong?"

"I don't think so, but I only just ran a home pregnancy test this morning."

He closed the steps between them. "You're two

months along and just figured it out today? You haven't even been to a doctor?"

She fought the urge to stand and jab him in the chest. She would probably just faint at his feet again anyway. "Don't raise your voice at me."

He snorted on a laugh. "Now that's a switch. Usually you're the one shouting."

"Sit down and listen, please." She waited until he took his seat beside her, which placed his thigh and arms temptingly against hers.

Marianna swallowed hard and forged ahead. "I know it sounds strange, but at first, I couldn't bring myself to believe I'm actually finally pregnant."

"That's what you wanted to talk to me about next week."

"Yes, once I had a chance to confirm it with a doctor."

She waited while he processed the information. This wasn't going nearly as badly as she'd feared. Maybe in spite of all the harsh and hurtful words they'd tossed at each other over the years, they could be civil when it came to their child.

Sebastian slid his arm along the back of the sofa, almost touching her shoulders. "I still don't understand one thing."

She fidgeted, trying to ignore the warmth of him moving closer. She could not, would not let hormones muddy the waters between them, peace and objectivity all the more important with their child's happiness in the balance. "What's that?"

"If you took a pregnancy test this morning, why didn't you tell me before the final divorce decree?"

Everything went still inside her until her pulse grew all the louder in contrast. So much for hoping this would go well.

She should have known he wouldn't let that part pass, and maybe his driven persistence was the very reason she hadn't told him. What if he'd tried to stop the proceedings? Her heart had been bruised enough by this man. She couldn't have withstood hearing him say he wanted to stay married for the baby, especially since he'd only married her in the first place because of an unplanned pregnancy.

"Sebastian, this doesn't change anything."

"Like hell it doesn't."

She rose, at the end of her tether and in need of distance. "I will be in touch with you after I see my doctor." She scooped up her portfolio and inched toward the door. "We have seven months left to settle visitation and child support."

Just that fast, he stood behind her at the door, his breath hot on her scalp. "That's not what I'm talking about. Do you really think I would have gone through with the divorce if you had told me?" He skimmed his knuckles along the back of her neck with a persuasive gentleness at odds with the terse edge to his words. "Or was that your intent all along in keeping this a secret? Making sure you could cut me out as much as possible?"

"That's not fair." Although she couldn't ignore

the grain of truth in what he'd said, she also knew she'd made the right choice. She turned to face him—and draw his enticing caress off her skin. "We were getting ready to contact divorce lawyers before when we heard about a baby girl coming up for adoption. We stayed together for Sophie, and it didn't make any difference. If anything, we grew farther apart afterward. I can't—I won't—go through that again."

"Don't—" He held up a hand, his face tight, cold. "Don't bring up her name just to derail this discussion."

Eight months ago, she would have given anything to share comfort with him while they grieved over Sophie being taken away without warning. But he'd shut down, shut her out, left her basically alone to deal with the most emotionally-crippling event in her life.

She'd learned to stand on her own and she couldn't sacrifice that hard-won ground now. "Oh, that's right, we can't talk about Sophie." Her voice cracked but she plowed ahead. "We have to pretend the child we both loved for four months doesn't even exist."

"Fighting over the past doesn't change the present." He neatly dodged mentioning Sophie's name yet again.

Marianna bit her lip until she tasted blood. Her chest heaved with emotion and the need to cry out her frustration. Was her well of tears bottomless after all? "Fine, you win on that one. I can't take any more stress today."

"I agree you need to stay calm. We have another more pressing issue anyway."

"What now?" She didn't have any reserves left to combat his doctor of jurisprudence skills at winning.

He reached for the doorknob, his other hand clamping gently but surely around her arm. "We're going to find Dr. Cohen."

She started to argue that she could find her own damn doctor when something he'd said earlier tickled through the anger to taunt her. She unpacked their conversation and realized, hey wait— He'd said he didn't carry condoms because they didn't need them, which led her to a heart-stuttering conclusion.

He didn't carry them because even with their divorce in the works, he hadn't been seeing anyone else.

"There's your baby." Dr. Cohen pointed to the ultrasound machine. "And that's a healthy heartbeat."

Sebastian stared at the screen, unable to take his eyes off the tiny bean shape wriggling around. His *child*. In no universe had he predicted his day would turn out this way. At best, he'd expected his brothers to pour vintage bourbon down his throat until he could pass out and sleep away his first night of renewed bachelorhood.

Not in his wildest dreams had he imagined

chasing down an ob-gyn at the courthouse and requesting she take a surprise drop-in client. And in the times he'd let himself consider the possibility of Marianna becoming pregnant, he definitely hadn't thought they would both work to avoid touching and looking at each other.

Dr. Cohen typed commands on the keyboard, the image on the screen freezing as she readjusted Marianna's gown and sheet. "And that's all for today." She patted Marianna's arm. "Once you get dressed, stop by my office on your way out."

Marianna's hands fisted in the crackly paper covering on the exam table. "Is something wrong?"

"Nothing that I can see." Dr. Cohen slid on her glittery red glasses and jotted notations on the chart before slapping it closed. "I need to give you your prescription for prenatal vitamins. And if you opt to stay with me as your ob-gyn, we need to set up your next appointment."

The ob-gyn reached beneath the monitor and came back with two black-and-white glossy photos. "A picture of the baby for both of you. Congratulations, Mom and Dad."

Marianna reached to grasp the doctor's hand. "Thank you for all your help and patience this afternoon. You've really gone above and beyond for us."

"I imagine this has been a roller-coaster day. I'm glad to be of help." Dr. Cohen pulled the privacy curtain aside, then in place again a second before the door clicked open and closed.

Marianna inched up, tucking the sheet around her. "Sebastian, could you please step outside?"

He tore his eyes from the photo to Marianna. The paper "blouse" and sheet strategically covered everything. But now that she mentioned it, he couldn't help but think of her bare beneath those flimsy barriers.

Her breasts seemed fuller—from the pregnancy?—tempting him to test their weight with his hands, explore the swell brought on from carrying his child. No matter how long they stayed apart, he would never forget the exact feel and shape of her.

He'd been her lover since they were eighteen years old. He'd become her husband when they found out she was pregnant. Interesting how life had a way of repeating itself.

"Sebastian—" Her indignant voice pulled him back into the sterile reality of the exam room.

"Relax, Marianna. I've seen you naked, and undoubtedly I'm going to see you that way again at future doctor visits. Then there's the delivery—"

"Stop. You may have rights when it comes to your baby—" she shoved her tousled curls out of her face "—but we're not married anymore, and that means no more naked fashion shows after I go shoe shopping."

"Damn shame." He plucked her slingbacks from the floor and set them on the exam table. "That's a hot pair of silver heels you're sporting."

She opened her mouth, and he held up both

hands, realizing he'd pushed his luck as far as he could for one day.

"I'm going. I'm going." For now. "I'll be waiting in the doctor's office."

He didn't expect they would return to the way things were, but he resented being dismissed so easily. In fact, he didn't intend to be dismissed from his child's life at all. He hadn't walked away from his responsibilities at eighteen, and he sure as hell didn't intend to at twenty-seven.

Marianna might not know it yet, but theirs was going to be one of the shortest divorces on record.

Marianna hadn't expected to end the day riding in Sebastian's Beemer, and she resented being here now. Already he was taking over her life again—the doctor, the half-eaten hoagie in her lap. And while they'd been at Dr. Cohen's, he'd arranged for his youngest brother, Jonah, to drive her car back to her house—their old home.

Sebastian had simply stated he worried about her becoming dizzy behind the wheel even though pregnant women drove every day. Although she had to admit, this day wasn't like any other. Surely when she woke in the morning she could take a calm moment to simply enjoy the photo of her baby, Sebastian's baby.

Moon battling the sun, she studied her ex-husband's stern profile as he drove past the golf course leading into the seaside subdivision where they'd built their two-story colonial dream house. Palmetto trees lined the road, marsh grass just beyond bordering the darkening seashore.

His family fortune and her inheritance from her parents had eased some of their earlier years when they both had been in college. Though they'd both rushed to graduate and start earning their own way. Maybe they would have split sooner if they'd been forced to struggle financially.

Marianna watched as they passed house after house, neighbor after neighbor. She'd been planning to move into a condo, away from memories. Now she didn't know where she would live. She had so many plans to revise.

Plans. For the first time since she'd risen this morning—and promptly tossed her cookies—she felt *happy*. She blinked back tears. "We're going to have a baby."

He cut his eyes toward her. "Appears so."

"I need some time for it to soak in. Then we can start making decisions." Like how she traveled to and from appointments and how much of her body he saw. "My work schedule is more flexible than yours. Let me know when you're free next week, and I'll be there."

"Thanks. And I'll have my accountant deposit money in your checking account tomorrow so you can put in your two weeks' notice."

She sat up bolt right. Surely he couldn't have meant what she thought. "What did you say?"

"You already miscarried once." He paused for a yield sign, calm-as-can-freaking-be, as if he hadn't just ordered her to quit her job. "You need to take things easy."

Stay cool. Try not to think about his jealousy of her boss in the past. They only had a few more yards until she could escape into the house. "That's for the doctor to decide, not you. And I lost the first baby because of an ectopic pregnancy. We already know from the ultrasound that isn't the case this time."

"I have enough money—more than enough—so you don't have to work." He charged ahead with his plan as if she hadn't spoken. "Why risk it?"

Flashbacks of that frightening miscarriage rolled through her head. How she and Sebastian had gone to the mountains for their honeymoon after eloping, both of them realizing their relationship was starting on shaky ground and hoping to cement their feelings with a getaway.

Instead, four days in, the excruciating pain and scary bleeding had started. Then she'd endured the interminably long drive down the mountain road to find a hospital. The surgeon had told her if they'd arrived an hour later, she could have hemorrhaged to death.

She understood full well how quickly things could go wrong.

Marianna gathered her portfolio off the floor mat. "This is the very reason I wanted to wait until next week to discuss anything with you."

"Seven days to line up your arguments."

"Seven days to shore up my defenses against being bullied."

"You're right." He glanced over at her with a curt nod. "You shouldn't be upset."

"I'll take that as an apology."

He stayed silent beside her, slowing the car to turn onto her street. He never apologized. After arguments, he analyzed how they could have chosen their words differently. He left extravagant gifts. He bought her a day at the spa.

But he never said those three magic words: *I am sorry*.

Staring into the night sky, Marianna blinked fast against the moisture stinging again. Sebastian put the car into Park outside their brick home with white columns and leaned across the seat. He pulled her close, and she let herself rest against his chest even if she didn't actually touch him back.

She sniffled, scrubbing her wrist over her damp eyes. "It's just the hormones, understand?"

"Got it." He gave her shoulders a quick squeeze then stepped out of the car.

She opened the passenger door, steeling her will to stop him at the steps. Marianna's hip bumped the door closed and she turned only to slam into Sebastian standing stone still. All tenderness left his face as he stared at the front porch—where her boss, Ross Ward, waited in a rocking chair.

Four

Blood steaming, Sebastian resisted the urge—just barely—to launch up the steps and pitch Ross Ward off the porch on his Italian-jean-clad ass. The bastard apparently wasn't wasting any time making his move on Marianna now that she was a free woman.

Boy, did Ward have a surprise coming his way.

But not now. Marianna had been through enough drama for one day, so Sebastian reined himself in. Hell, a divorce, surprise pregnancy and decision to win her back rocked even him on his heels.

Sebastian pivoted slowly to face her again,

sculpting control into his voice given her boss had been a sore subject between them in the past. "What's he doing here?"

"I have no idea." Marianna shrugged, hitching her portfolio under her arm and brushing by him toward their sprawling porch.

Ward shoved up from the white rocker, smoothing his casual jacket and tie. "What is *he* doing here?"

Sebastian had done his level best to be polite to the guy in the past. Her boss owned the interior decorator firm where she worked, after all. Ward handled the more masculine designs, making a name for himself as the decorator for sports stars across the Southeast. Marianna had been placed in charge of the homes for the *Southern Living* crowd.

He'd been okay with her boss at first, but over the years, he just couldn't get past the sense that Ward harbored feelings for Marianna. He even seemed to schedule her buying trips around the few times Sebastian had free.

His instincts had been validated often enough in the courtroom that he did not doubt himself for a second when it came to Marianna's boss.

Sebastian kept his hand on her shoulder as they walked along the decorative stepping stones winding around patches of flowers and a stone bird feeder. "Why am *I* here? I'm Marianna's husband."

"Ex-husband." Ward lounged against the porch column with a proprietary air that set Sebastian's teeth on edge. "I thought Marianna might need some cheering up after court." He stroked his close-trimmed blond beard as he faced her. "I've made dinner reservations. If we leave now, we can make still make it."

"Oh," she responded, looking flustered for the first time since they'd stepped from the car, "thank you—"

A low bark sounded from inside the house, growing louder and louder until a thud sounded on the other side of the door. Buddy. Marianna hurried past, and Sebastian wanted to dispense of this poaching jerk and go about normal life—walking on the beach with Marianna and talking about their baby, while their dogs bounded through the surf. And yeah, he was being semi-delusional given the workload weighing down his briefcase since he'd been forced to take half a day off for handling the mess his personal life had become.

Sebastian stopped on the porch, topping Ward by at least two inches. "She's already had supper."

Hanging baskets of ferns creaked in the evening breeze as Ward glanced at the half-eaten hoagie in Marianna's hand with ill-disguised disdain. "So I see."

She placed the sandwich on the rocker and unlocked the front door. Buddy bounded out as she knelt to greet the pug-faced mutt. "Hey there, fella. Did you miss me? I missed you—yes, I did."

Marianna adored that dog and by God, so did he.

An image blindsided him of a little girl one day dressing Buddy up in a tutu, and damn, but the mental vision sucker punched him hard.

He was a father again.

The reality of it rolled over him fully for the first time in a day that had moved too fast to let him think. All his lawyerly impulses revved to maximum velocity. He had a case to put forward, a family to win back. Losing was not an option.

Marianna rubbed her face against the dog's short fur, pitching her portfolio onto the hall floor, the long stairway up to the bedrooms beckoning. She reached to grab Buddy's leash draped over the rocker.

Sebastian quirked a brow at Ward. "Looks to me like she's settling in at home. Guess you'd better pull out your little black book and find someone else to share your grilled grouper."

"Hell-O." Marianna waved her hand between them, holding on to Buddy's leash as the dog leapt toward Sebastian. "I'm here, and I can speak for myself."

Ward stepped back from the bounding dog—all twenty-five pounds of "threatening" energy. "Of course you can. You're a single woman now."

Kneeling to scratch Buddy's neck, Sebastian didn't even bother holding back his smile over sharing this with Marianna. As much as they enjoyed their dogs, how much more awesome would it be when they saw their child for the first time? A connection that could never be broken.

Sebastian looked at her stomach, then over at Ward who was busy wiping dog drool off his Prada penny loafers. What would the guy think of Marianna's pregnancy?

She jabbed her finger in the middle of Sebastian's chest. "Don't even think about saying it."

He leaned over Buddy to whisper in her ear. "Shouldn't your boss know?"

She hissed between gritted teeth, "When I'm good and ready. You would be wise to remember it's in your best interest to stay in my good graces."

He didn't think for a minute that Marianna would keep his baby from him, but he wanted the whole package—wife and kid. This called for diplomacy on his part.

Ward looked from one to the other, his smugness faltering for the first time. "Was there some hitch in the proceedings?"

Marianna passed Buddy's leash over to Sebastian and turned to Ward. "The divorce is official." She stepped closer, a smile curving her soft lips. "Thank you for the dinner offer—that was thoughtful— but how about a rain check? I'm really tired."

Concern for her health mixed with relief over Ward being given his walking papers. As she escorted Ward to his low-slung Jaguar, Sebastian looped the leash around his hand, remembering late-night walks on the beach, memorable, but not all that frequent now that he thought back.

Juggling his workload while winning Marianna

over would be difficult, but then he'd always thrived on a challenge at work. And who needed sleep anyway?

The Jag's growling engine drew Sebastian's attention back to the manicured lawn and Marianna coming up the decorative stepping stones she'd picked out. She'd asked his opinion, but he left that sort of thing to her. She'd chosen well.

Marianna flattened a hand to a fat column. "Thank you for not saying anything about the baby. I'm not ready to tell the world yet. I need time for the news to settle in and some reassurance the pregnancy will go to term."

"Understood." The thought of her miscarrying again—the hell of her almost hemorrhaging to death all those years ago—clenched through him. And he refused to think of the daughter they'd lost a few short months ago. He couldn't even bring himself to think her name with the fresh slice those two syllables would bring.

Marianna scraped a fingernail along a smudge on the pillar with undue concentration. "Would you please hold off on telling your family?"

"I think it's something we should do together. But whenever you're ready." It was an easy enough concession, especially since his goal was keeping her even-keeled.

Confusion shadowed through her eyes in the dim porch light. "I can't believe how reasonable you're being about all this. That means a lot to me."

"Your peace of mind is my number one priority."

She looked down and away. "Of course. The baby's wellbeing comes first."

He skimmed knuckles along her arm. "I still care about you, too." And he meant it. He wanted her. Even though she seemed to have some pie-in-the-sky idea of what he should be able to give her, they had made some amazing memories together. That and their baby would be enough this time. It had to be. "It's impossible not to care after nine years of marriage."

She trembled under his touch, her pupils widening with desire as she rocked toward him. How damn ironic that it took a divorce to soften Marianna, but he wasn't one to squander an advantage. His hand slid up her arm to cup her neck—

Headlights swept the driveway as Ward pulled in behind Sebastian's Beemer. "Marianna? I meant to remind you before I left. Don't forget we're meeting with Matthew Landis and his fiancée tomorrow to discuss decorating plans for their new home."

Sebastian eased his hand away. So much for drop-kicking Ward to the curb just yet. But at least Sebastian knew exactly where he needed to be for supper tomorrow night.

The next evening, Marianna drove along the winding paved drive leading to the Landis compound. Palm trees and sea grass parted to reveal a white three-story house with Victorian peaks over-looking the ocean. A lengthy set of stairs stretched upward to the second-level wraparound porch that housed the main living quarters. Latticework shielded most of the first floor, which boasted a large entertainment area.

The attached garage held a fleet of expensive cars for all the family members residing in various suites and the carriage house. She stopped her Mercedes convertible out front by a clump of pink azaleas, having months ago handed over the garage remote she'd been given.

Although exhausted from a long afternoon deal-ing with a picky society scion with questionable taste, she looked forward to finishing her day here. She genuinely liked Sebastian's brother and his fiancée. She'd asked them repeatedly if they would prefer another decorator from Ross's business, and they'd insisted she was their first choice.

Climbing the stairway leading up to the main entrance, she reminded herself not to be nervous about seeing everyone. She was a twenty-seven-year-old woman with a successful career. She'd redecorated everything from a historic mayoral mansion to an elaborate tree house featured in *Architectural Digest*. She'd consulted on a design show that had been picked up in several regional markets. Besides, her ex-in-laws were wonderful people. They wouldn't skewer her just because she'd initiated the divorce.

She hoped.

Shuffling the portfolio packed with color swatches and sketches of room designs, Marianna started to grab the doorknob—then pulled her hand back as if burned. She wasn't family anymore. With a twinge to her heart, she rang the bell. She just wanted to get through this evening without tapping into more of those hormonal tears that seemed to hover ever-near.

The door swung wide to reveal her ex-mother-in-law, a smoothly beautiful woman with gray-blond hair. In her jeans and a short sleeve sweater set with pearls, no one would guess Ginger was one of the country's most powerful politicians.

Even having been a Landis for nine years, Marianna still found herself taken aback on occasion by so much financial and political power in one family. Sebastian's independently wealthy father had been a U.S. senator, a seat that passed to his wife after his premature death. Now that Ginger was on a short list to be the next secretary of state, her oldest son was running for her soon-to-be vacated senatorial spot.

Ginger wrapped Marianna in a warm hug and urged her inside. "Come in, dear." She smiled openly, easing some of the awkwardness. "You must be feeling better. You look positively radiant."

Pregnancy glow? Awkwardness tingled right back up Marianna's spine again.

"Uh, thank you, Ginger." Her shaky voice echoed up into the cathedral ceiling.

Ginger led her past the main living room, the wall of windows showcasing the stars just beginning to twinkle. Hardwood floors were scattered with light Persian rugs around two Queen Anne sofas upholstered in a pale blue fabric with white piping. Wingback chairs in a creamy yellow angled off the side in a formal but airy, comfortable way.

Marianna considered the decor one of her best works since she'd seen firsthand how the family worked and designed it with their needs in mind.

Ginger squeezed her elbow. "We're having dessert on the balcony. I saved a plate for you. I know chocolate cheesecake's your favorite."

As much as Marianna wanted to keep this businesslike, no mealtime chitchat, her first official pregnancy craving walloped her. She would have walked across nails for a slice of cheesecake. "That was very thoughtful of you."

Ginger paused just before the French balcony doors. "Even though you and Sebastian are no longer married, we still love you." She'd said the same before, but hearing it again after the divorce meant a lot, especially with the baby on the way. Even more so *because* Ginger didn't know about the baby. "You were my daughter for nine years and that's not something I can just shrug off."

Whoops, there went those hormonal tears after all as she studied Ginger with a new perspective—as her baby's grandmother. Why couldn't this have been a happy time of celebration? Heaven knew, she and Sebastian had dreamed often enough of the day they would be able to present Ginger with grandchildren.

They'd experienced this beautiful moment when Sophie joined their family at two days old.

Another tear slipped down her cheek. "I don't know what to say except thank you, and you're all very special to me, too."

Ginger whipped a tissue from a brass box on a cherry wood accent table. "I'm relieved to hear that."

Dabbing her eyes dry, Marianna prepared to face the rest of the group, hoping they would be as welcoming. Ginger swung the glass doors wide to the balcony overlooking the organic pool and rolling ocean.

As an only child, Marianna still felt overwhelmed by Sebastian's relatives at times, even in partial force. The second-born son, Kyle, was serving in the Air Force and had just been deployed to Afghanistan. She scanned the porch, the wicker furniture full of Sebastian's family.

The General, Sebastian's stepfather, slid an arm around Ginger's shoulders and smiled his welcome to Marianna. "We're glad to have a chance to see you before we head back to D.C."

The older Air Force pilot now served on the Joint Chiefs of Staff. Ginger and Hank Renshaw divided their time between South Carolina and the nation's capital.

Sebastian's oldest brother, Matthew, sat at a small corner table with his fiancée, Ashley; the engaged couple feeding each other cheesecake in such a blatant display of love Marianna clenched the damp tissue in her fist.

"Hey, Marianna," the youngest of the Landis brothers, Jonah, said as he flipped a lock of shaggy hair off his brow. Tossing a mint into the air, he bounced it off his head and into his mouth with the seasoned dexterity of a college soccer player. Except now he'd graduated, and he was busy "finding" himself.

A bark drew her attention to the beach to see Holly—running with Sebastian.

He'd left work early? Blinking back her surprise, she allowed herself a second to study him playing Frisbee with their other dog—his dog now. He'd even been home long enough to change into khaki shorts and a polo shirt.

She braced herself for the inevitable wave of attraction. Wind ruffled his brown hair as he sprinted with a lean, athletic grace. What kind of craziness was this that she ached for his body even more now than before the divorce? Was this some kind of weird quirk of nature along the lines of want but can't have?

Or could it be another by-product of the hormonal flood assaulting her system?

Matthew Landis rose from his chair, his hand still resting affectionately on his shy fiancée's shoulder. "Thanks for coming over, Marianna. Hope you don't mind if we look at the plans out here."

As much as she wanted to retreat away from the lure of family life, who could argue with this million-dollar view? The *beach* view that was, not Sebastian, blast it.

Marianna kept her mind focused on business, doing her best to avoid the magnetic pull of her tanned ex thudding up the steps. "I'm glad to be here. Ross will be joining us shortly. He got held up by an accident on one of the bridges."

"Hey, beautiful." Sebastian's voice drifted up the stairs.

An awkward silence settled like a storm cloud on the otherwise clear evening. Holly bounded past him, breaking the tension and providing her with a welcome alternative focus.

Marianna met Holly halfway down the wooden stairs, needing a chance to break the ice with Sebastian before facing him with his whole family in earshot. "You're off work early."

"A guy's gotta eat sometime."

She restrained herself from mentioning how many meals he'd taken at his desk. Was he genuinely making an effort because of the baby? If so, only time would tell whether or not he could maintain the change.

Marianna knelt to rub Holly's ears. The brown-and-black mutt rolled onto her back appreciatively. God, she missed the sweetie and questioned again the wisdom of separating the two dogs. Had she been selfish? Should she have let them stay together with Sebastian? She had given them both to him for Christmas two years ago, after all.

Warm, strong fingers banded around her ankle and she, startled, found herself eye level with Sebastian. His thumb slid between her high heel and foot to stroke her arch, a spot he knew full well to be an erogenous zone.

"Nice shoes." He tapped the strap on her fire-engine-red heels—and no, she hadn't chosen them with him in mind.

Had she?

She inched her foot free, the exact imprint of his fingers still tingling along her bare skin. She wanted more, ached to test the rasp of his five o'clock shadow along the sensitive pads of her fingers. Gauging by the knowing glint in his blue eyes, he understood exactly what he was doing to her.

Marianna leaned closer, whispering, "Touch me that way again and the heel goes through your hand."

"You sure don't pull any punches." He tugged a lock of her dark hair, stroking his fingers down its length and finishing with a gentle pull.

"You're a big boy. You can handle it." She eased her head away from his tempting caress. Too easily she could be wooed by the warmth of his touch and the welcome of his family.

"Can *you* handle it?" His hand grazed hers under the guise of petting Holly.

"Do I even want to?"

"You tell me." His warm blue eyes turned lazy. "The Beemer's out front."

She swatted his hand aside, all too aware of his family working overly hard at conversation on the porch. "Stop flirting."

"'Scuse me. Were you talking?" His gaze fell to her chest. "I was busy checking out your new curves."

She rolled her eyes, sighing, not sure whether to be miffed or charmed by his teasing. At least he was trying in his own way to smooth over this awkward moment.

Regardless, she wasn't sure how much more of his sensual teasing she *could* handle tonight. Marianna climbed back up the steps just as Ross Ward strode onto the balcony in his signature jeans and jacket.

Sebastian palmed her back.

Frustration simmered low, battling with the urge to press more firmly against his hand. Hadn't she just told him to stop touching her? She looked over her shoulder at her ex and found he wasn't looking her way at all. His eyes were narrowed and locked firmly on Ross.

Damn. So much for her hopeful thoughts of a pleasant evening with a reformed Sebastian. Her ex-husband hadn't changed in the least.

Sebastian was marking his territory.

Five

Sebastian was in the doghouse and he knew it. He'd been there often enough in the past to recognize the signs of Marianna's fast blinking and tight lips. But having been intimately acquainted with the inside of said doghouse provided the handy benefit of knowing how to get back out.

Marianna had a temper, no question, but she also usually had a forgiving heart. Yet somewhere along the line in their marriage, he'd stopped caring about making up and she'd stopped caring that he didn't try anymore.

Tonight, however, with a baby to consider, he decided it was time to capitalize on those old making-up skills with a walk along the beach. He just needed to persuade her to join in before she had time to fish out her keys and climb into her Mercedes.

She'd been ticked off with him since her hippie boss had arrived. Not that anyone else would have noticed. Sebastian had gone through the motions of a pleasant dessert meeting, pretending interest as Matthew and Ashley chose the decor for the home they were having built.

Sebastian was genuinely interested in seeing his brother and happy new fiancée, of course, but he didn't know squat about decorating. He spent most of the evening trying to pinpoint what it was about Ward that set off his protective radar. Yet no matter how closely he watched the guy, there was never anything overt. Ward didn't touch Marianna too much, was always deferential to her opinions and eager to hear what she had to say.

About a year ago, he'd tried to spell out his concerns about the guy to Marianna and she'd about blown a gasket explaining that just because Sebastian never wanted to have a conversation didn't mean every man felt the same way. This proved, once again, that her boss was a topic they couldn't discuss rationally.

Now as Ward drove down the driveway, Sebastian stood with Marianna outside her convertible prepping his strategy to divert her anger before it erupted into an argument. "Let's let Holly run for a few minutes so we can talk away from my family."

She was always on him about spending too much time at work and not enough time relaxing together. A walk should fit the bill.

He kept his hands in his pockets. She wouldn't be receptive to touches yet, not until she cooled down. With stars winking overhead, the backdrop of the opaque night ocean would set the romantic mood well enough.

Hesitating, she twisted her key ring. She didn't look quite ready to forget her anger…

Finally, she nodded an acceptance of his offer and tossed her keys on top of her portfolio on the front seat. Nobody would steal her car inside the gated confines of the Landis family compound. "A walk sounds nice. I should start getting more exercise, and there's something I need to discuss with you."

Yeah, he figured as much, but he would sidetrack her before she had a chance to start that "Ross Ward Fight" again.

She picked her way alongside him, heels sinking into the sandy lawn as he circled the main house toward the beach. Sea oats rustled in the distance along with the gush and roar of the waves on the shore. Holly bounded ahead and into the surf, the more playful of their pets. He'd been insistent on Marianna keeping Buddy because of the dog's protectiveness.

Thinking of Marianna alone in the big house...

Sebastian stuffed down thoughts certain to frustrate him at a time he needed to keep his cool more than ever. It proved to be a tough enough job already with her exotic perfume scenting the breeze, reminding him of times that same scent clung to their sheets.

Marianna kicked off her shoes and jogged ahead to join their dog. Her short suit skirt left plenty of leg bare to splash through the waves, her hair tumbling down her back. The wind plastered her untucked blouse to her breasts with an intimacy his hands ached to copy.

He scooped up her heels and watched. She'd gone from angry to laughing in the span of two minutes all because of a pup's playfulness. Marianna's exuberance entranced him. How long had it been since that happened? A few years into their marriage, he'd become irritated with her distractibility, no longer seeing the charm of her capricious moods.

As if she felt his eyes on her, she glanced back over her shoulder and stopped. Her arms fell to her sides again, moonlight playing with all those different shades of brown in her hair.

Tiny sand crabs scuttled past his feet as her smile faded. Once again she wore her defensive cloak of awareness from their past fights. Countless times he'd asked her to stay on topic while she demanded he quit using his lawyer logic on her and shout back, damn it. The past threatened to suck him under again with its old numbing anger at a time *he* needed to stay on topic. Maybe he should slip off his own shoes and—

"All right." Marianna approached him and said, "What do you need to say now that we're away from your family?"

He wanted the dancing Marianna back. "Is it a crime to spend time together?"

"We're divorced, not dating." She began walking at least, if not dancing.

He eased closer to her side as they left the house farther behind. "We have to establish neutral ground before the baby is born. Tension isn't good for a kid."

"I agree," she conceded graciously—then her eyes sparked with renewed anger as bright as the starlight in the clear black sky. "I just don't want you to think this child provides you with a magical key to resume our marriage."

Were his plans that damn transparent? And what happened to her anger about Ross Ward? "What makes you believe I want to remarry so soon after the kick-in-the-teeth of a divorce?"

Her eyebrows pinched together, her lips pursing into a bow he burned to nip. "Sebastian, do you realize that's the first time you've expressed any kind of emotional feelings regarding the divorce?"

"What kind of robot goes through something like that without being affected?"

She stayed silent, giving him his answer with a

shocking clarity. He was about to explode into flames from wanting this woman and she really *did* see him as some kind of emotionless machine. He might not shout and pitch a fortune in crystal and dishes but he felt things. He just didn't waste energy ruminating about them.

"Marianna, let's get back to what you said before…" and crap, he'd just fallen into his old habit of steering things on topic. Too late now to change course, though. "Why would you assume I've already got a new wedding-ring set tucked and waiting in my pocket?"

"The last time I got pregnant, you insisted on doing the 'right' thing and I want to make sure you understand this is different."

"We were in love then."

She sure hadn't labeled him a robot in those early days.

"Love?" Marianna stumbled, and he caught her elbow before she could trip to her knees in the surf. "I, uh, didn't expect you to be this understanding of the difference between now and then."

"Did you want me to fight for you?" Of course, this was what he was doing. She just didn't know it. Yet.

"No, no, of course not." She scraped her wind-swept hair from her face to reveal her confusion. "I only thought that with the baby… I don't know what I thought anymore. Except that I don't under-stand why you went all green-eyed monster with

Ross again. He's just a friend, but even if it was more, we're divorced."

A friend? Sebastian didn't doubt for a minute the man wanted to be a helluva lot more. What did Marianna want? "Are you planning to go out with him?" He held up his hands before she could go on the defensive. "I'm honestly just curious."

She wrapped her arms around her waist, emphasizing her lush new curves. "I'm planning to have a baby."

"Pregnant women date, and I'm absolutely certain you will be one of the sexiest pregnant women on the planet."

She glanced up at him through her lashes. "You're flirting again."

"I'm stating the obvious." And he'd probably pushed as hard as he could for one night. It was time for a strategic step back in the interest of staying on track with his real goal—getting a ring on her finger before the pale patch of skin had time to tan over.

He didn't have the new diamond bought yet—even he wasn't that organized—but he didn't intend to let grass grow under his feet while he waited around. "I realize the marriage is over," he lied, but hey, he was a lawyer after all. "Still, I hope that we can use these next few months to rebuild our friendship. For the baby's sake, of course."

Stopping, she toyed with her untucked blouse grazing over her stomach. "No more nitpicking me to death about Ross?"

Any other time he would have pressed that point, but right now was about slipping into Marianna's good graces, then back into her life. "I hear you and will do my level best to lock away all caveman tendencies."

She laughed lightly and picked up her pace along the water's edge again, heading toward the house. Well, damn, her temper could be diffused that easily? Either he'd missed the boat in the past or pregnancy hormones had mellowed her.

He slowed his strides to stay even with her as they walked through the ebb and flow of the tide, time passing in a semicomfortable silence. He wanted to kiss her, lower her to the sand behind a dune and celebrate their baby news the good old-fashioned way, but no doubt even a hint of that would only cut the walk short. For now, he would settle for this slice of time with Marianna that felt like a replay of their early days together.

Too soon they were nearing the house.

Marianna tipped her face into the wind. "This isn't the way I expected things to be after we divorced. When do you think we will start fighting?"

"I hope no time soon, but I'm not counting on it." He scooped up a piece of driftwood and tossed it ahead for Holly.

"That's a fair assumption. Especially if you keep talking about me quitting work."

"So warned."

She stopped on the beach, waves lapping around

her ankles. "Thank you for suggesting this. You were right. It was a nice way to unwind after work."

"I wish I had taken the time to do it more often." And this time he wasn't lying.

Her eyes widened with surprise. She opened her mouth a couple of times as if searching for words before she finally said, "I should leave now."

It was time to shift off serious footing before she resurrected the walls. "Aw, aren't you going to walk me to my door?"

"You've got to be kidding."

"I feel so cheap."

"Sebastian…" she warned, but a hint of laughter softened her scowl.

He passed Marianna her shoes. "Now *that* was flirting."

Smiling, she snagged her heels from him. "You do it well."

"Thanks." He would have offered to walk her to her car, but she was safe enough on the secured property and he needed to run off the edginess from being so close to her yet being unable to touch her the way he wanted. "You go on ahead. Holly needs to exercise for a while longer."

"Good night, Sebastian." She leaned down to give their dog a final ear ruffle—and provide him with a too clear and tormenting view down the front of her blouse before she straightened. Waving as she turned away, she picked along the shore those last few yards toward the house.

Watching the sweet sway of her hips proved a double-edged sword. The sight completely rocked his socks, but he would have to run at least a couple of miles if he planned to sleep at all tonight.

He snagged another piece of driftwood and turned to Holly. "Hey, girl, are you ready to race?"

The mutt leapt higher, trying to snag the wood from his hand. He arced his hand back, ready for a long pitch—

A scream cut the air and clean through him. That wasn't just any scream.

It was Marianna.

Marianna barely had time to hop on one foot out of the surf before Sebastian sprinted up beside her. He scooped her into his arms, not even panting, yet sweat dotted his brow. "What's wrong? Is it the baby?"

No wonder he'd broken into a cold sweat. She squeezed his shoulder reassuringly and tried to resist the temptation of sinking deeper into his hot, muscled arms. "I'm all right. I just got stung by a jellyfish."

It hurt like a son-of-a-gun, but the hard play of Sebastian's flexing biceps under her hand offered a welcome distraction. The tense furrows on his face eased somewhat but not completely as he carried her up the incline and past the white-iron fence into the patio area. He lowered her to sit on the edge of the pool, submerging her calf in the cool water for a few soothing seconds before pulling it back out to examine.

Sebastian cradled her foot in his hand, turning it from side to side and studying the slight pink color of her skin around her ankle. "Let's go inside, and I'll get something to take the fire out."

She wasn't heading back into the warm and wonderfully welcoming Landis home. Especially not on an evening when she was already too weakened by memories of the good times they'd shared, recollections she'd somehow forgotten over the past couple of years as the chill had settled deeper and deeper into her marriage.

"It's not that bad. The sting is already fading, and the water really helps." She lowered her foot into the pool again. "I bet if I sit here for a couple of minutes I'll be fine to drive home."

He eyed the house, then her, the wheels of his logical brain almost visibly turning. The remaining tension finally eased from him, and he took off his shoes as well.

Now that was a shocker.

Then he lowered his feet into the pool. Who was this man, and what had he done with her brooding ex-husband?

His leg brushed against hers and all distracting thoughts took flight on the next gust of wind, leaving her free to focus only on the sensation of his skin against hers. His thigh teased her with each tantalizingly brief swish. An ache settled low inside her that had nothing to with the jellyfish burn and everything to do with the man beside her.

Damn him for reminding her of things she'd enjoyed about him before, of happier times. And she couldn't even blame him because still she sat here beside him, swaying closer. Her body had been weak willed around this man since she was eighteen years old.

His shoulders seemed even larger, if possible, shaded by the darkness of the seashore behind him. She waited, transfixed by a desire greater than she wanted or needed with him again.

Sebastian's hands slid from the edge of the pool onto her head, his fingers trailing along her hair. Her eyes drifted closed as his touch brushed down. He clasped her shoulders, pulling her against his broad chest, anchoring her with the caressing pressure of one palm.

Grasping her hair in his other hand, he wrapped its length around his wrist and tipped her head back with a gentle tug. The light sting echoed the tingle in her breasts pressed against him. She gasped in surprise when his lips skimmed her exposed neck, nipped her earlobe and grazed her cheekbone before hovering over her mouth. He gave her hair a more forceful tug until her lids flickered open.

"What the—" Sebastian jolted as Holly nudged between them. He gripped the mutt by the collar.

She slumped against him, gasping in hot humid gulps of sea air, relief and regret jockeying for control inside her. "Holly just saved us both from making a big mistake."

Sebastian didn't confirm or deny her statement, just stared back at her, his eyes flecked with the flinty blue she only saw during sex. Regardless of any regrets, she knew what she had to do.

Marianna angled away from him, snagging her shoes. If they'd kissed much longer, she would have been following him…anywhere. In fact, with the flush of desire still hot on her skin, she couldn't race back to her car fast enough.

Gasping, Sebastian bolted upright on the leather sofa in his office. He swiped an arm over his sweat-drenched face and swung his feet to the carpeted floor. At least he didn't have to worry about Marianna chewing him out for working too late—again.

Reaching down, he rubbed his mutt behind the ears. He wasn't sure why he'd brought Holly with him when he'd come into work after his walk with Marianna. He'd never done it before. For some reason it just seemed the thing to do when Holly had barked at the door as he headed for his car at ten in the evening.

"Hey, girl." Rough as freshly laid gravel, his voice scratched the air.

He eyed the grandfather clock in the corner—three o'clock in the morning. He'd only been asleep for an hour—long enough to sink into the night-marish night nine years ago when he'd driven Marianna down the mountain pass to the hospital, scared as hell she would die before he could get her help. And during the whole seemingly endless drive, kicking himself for choosing such a remote locale for a getaway with his *pregnant* new wife.

The scent of mountain air and her perfume still clung to his senses. How many times would he have to relive it in his sleep? Maybe Marianna was right, and they really were flat-out wrong for each other.

Sebastian rose, working the kink from his neck that had been there long before he slept on the sofa, and lumbered through down the dim hall and into the small kitchenette without pausing to flip a switch. Why bother? There wasn't much risk of bumping into anybody at the firm at this time of night.

And he spent enough time here that he had the layout memorized.

He opened the refrigerator door, the slim light knifing through the darkness. He plucked out a leftover foam container from his favorite rib restaurant—a place that knew him well after he and Marianna split. They even regularly delivered him meals after closing. One hip resting against the sink, Sebastian lifted the lid and pulled out a dry cold rib, picked it clean, tossed the bone to Holly, then started the unsatisfying process over again. More from habit than hunger, Sebastian ate, all the while thinking about the ultrasound photo in his wallet.

Sebastian threw Holly another bone. "Little different than how things used to be, huh, girl?"

There had been good times, damn it.

Sifting through the leftover dinner, he scavenged up a memory to replace the nightmare. Nearly two years ago, Marianna had surprised him at Christmas with the pair of puppies. How could he forget the power of her infectious smile as she set loose both boisterous animals with red bows around their necks, complete with adoption papers from the local animal shelter?

Sebastian looked down at the now full-grown mutt with her pug face and terrier body. Holly growled as she gnawed a bone, and he could almost hear Marianna giving him hell for feeding the dog table scraps.

She'd been right tonight about the divorce not playing out the way either of them could have predicted. Their whole marriage hadn't played out the way they expected, first with the miscarriage and then with losing Sophie.

Damn. He cut that pathway to more of the doubts that had led him to divorce court in the first place. He had to stay focused. Life had changed directions, and that was a fact—accept it and deal with it. He had a baby on the way now, and he wasn't going to be a long-distance dad.

And he sure as hell wasn't going to turn over his child to be raised by some guy like Ross Ward.

Wooing Marianna was a solid place to start. But if that didn't work, he would resort to any means necessary. Nightmares be damned, the stakes were just too high to waste time on anything less than a full press ahead.

Six

Tossing and turning all night from dreams of making love with Sebastian on the beach had left Marianna tired, cranky. And late for work. Her bout of morning sickness hadn't helped her stay on schedule either. Juggling her portfolio and sacked breakfast she hoped to be able to eat now that her stomach had settled, Marianna opened her office door only to stop short.

Sebastian was sprawled on her Queen Anne, Jacobin print sofa—asleep.

She started across the room to boot him off her couch and out of her office. What if her boss walked in? Or the receptionist?

Why couldn't Sebastian understand they weren't married anymore? He didn't have the right to waltz in and out of her life at his leisure. He needed to call in advance, make an appointment.

Dropping her portfolio and insulated food bag onto a wingback chair, she stopped inches away from his propped leather loafers. Had they really come to a place in their lives where they needed to schedule a time to talk? How damn sad.

Marianna snagged a tissue from the silver box on the end table and polished a scuff off the tip of his shoe, her eyes traveling up his toned long legs in a slightly rumpled suit. It wasn't fair that her body should be raging with hormones that left her achy and wanting at a time when Sebastian was officially forbidden territory.

Her eyes scanned along the taut muscles of his chest, suit coat parted as his hand lay on the floor. Then her gaze reached his face. Taut lines along the corners of his eyes and his jaw showed his exhaustion. From too much work? Would he continue this pace after their baby was born?

Old instincts stirred inside her, concern for how hard he pushed himself mixed with frustration at his uncompromising ways. She tried to tell herself she only cared because he was the father of her child, but couldn't ignore the extra twinge to her heart. Her feelings for him weren't as easily cast aside as she had thought while pursuing the divorce in her numbed state of grief.

She thought about waking him—but reconsid-ered. Let him sleep. She had plenty of work to keep her busy. And, yes, maybe she was trying to prove something to herself by staying in the room with him and successfully stifling the urge to stroke the stress lines from his forehead.

Marianna settled into the wingback, her feet on the ottoman. She spread an antique auction catalog open on her lap while she peeled back the foil top from her yogurt.

Fifteen minutes and a carton of boring dairy goop later, the grandfather clock in the corner chimed eleven o'clock. Sebastian startled awake, gripping the side of the sofa to keep from pitching off.

"Hi there, gorgeous." He scrubbed a hand over his face, his gravelly voice sounding too tempt-ingly like numerous shared mornings over the years. "How are you feeling?"

"We're doing fine." She smiled, placing the cata-log on the ground beside her. "Just putting my feet up for breakfast and a little professional reading."

He sat at the end of the Queen Anne sofa, scooped up her feet and swung them to rest in his lap. She started to protest, but then he pressed his thumbs into her arches and she had to focus all her energy on not moaning in ecstasy. "The pregnancy books say you should get plenty of rest."

She tried not to bristle at him stating the obvious. She wasn't the scatterbrained artsy eighteen-year-old he'd married. "I'm not likely to forget since you texted me instructions often enough yesterday."

Sebastian leaned forward, angling close to her stomach. "Your mama's getting feisty, so she must be feeling good."

"Actually, I'm still hungry." Which perhaps accounted for her irritability. Eating healthy sucked when her body screamed for other treats—edible as well as sexual. "Do you fully comprehend the power of an estrogen-induced craving?"

"It just so happens, I brought you dessert."

"Thanks, but I already ate and I want to be careful about eating healthy," she said as her sweet tooth ached.

"Lady, I've known you for nine years and that includes the foods you prefer. As a matter of fact, the way you enjoy your food is more than a little hot."

A tingle of awareness spread from her feet and up her legs at a time when her heated dreams were still too close to the surface. "So you like the way I pig out."

"Put your feet up again, and I'll surprise you with a brunch you'll never forget."

He reached over the arm of the sofa and pulled up a canvas shopping bag. One at a time, he set out an array of plastic containers filled with strawberries and kiwi and pear slices. She pressed her lips tight to hold back her frown.

The fruit looked beautiful, but she really wanted

a slice of fudge. Or, hey, maybe a Milky Way. Didn't that at least *sound* healthy since it contained the word *milk?*

Since he'd obviously tried, she forced a smile on her face, reminding herself of the stash of mini-pralines in her desk drawer. They had nuts and that equaled protein. "This was really thoughtful of you."

He'd taken great care to make sure the baby had exactly what it needed.

"And last but not least, we have…" He pulled out a jar.

"Peanut butter?" she asked, more than a little disappointed. Couldn't he have at least gotten her some peanut butter truffles?

"My dear, this is white chocolate raspberry peanut butter."

Her mouth watered while her heart fluttered with a scary hint of softening over the romantic thoughtfulness directed at *her.* "Really?"

He pulled out another. "And café mocha peanut butter. Last but not least, coconut-banana flavored." He winked. "Stay in good with me and I'll hook you up with the gourmet section in the all-night store where I found this to slather on your fruit."

Suddenly the strawberries looked a helluva lot more enticing. She grabbed for the jar. "Pass it over pronto, big guy."

He held the peanut butter out of her reach and opened the lid with one of those smooth male moves. Such a simple domestic thing—can you open this jar for me?—but it tweaked at her already-vulnerable heart. He pulled out a silver butter knife and smoothed some of the white chocolate raspberry peanut butter onto a fat strawberry.

She thought for a moment that he would try to feed it to her, and she would have to draw a line at a time when she really just wanted to enjoy the moment. Then he speared the strawberry with a toothpick and passed it over.

Marianna bit the treat in half, the juicy taste of fruit and chocolate exploding over her taste buds in a near-orgasmic flood. Her eyes fluttered closed so she could shut out all distracting sensations and focus fully on the intense flavor. She *so* didn't care about those truffles anymore.

She bit at the rest of the strawberry, but it bobbled on the toothpick. Sebastian reached at the same time she did, their fingers meeting at her lips.

Glinting blue eyes locked with hers. His gaze fell to her mouth, her breath coming faster. Marianna's thumb twitched as if trying of its own volition to connect with Sebastian. Then she snatched her hand away.

Sebastian relaxed back onto the sofa, surprising her when he didn't relentlessly push for more. They had nearly kissed last night, yet he seemed willing to respect her boundaries now.

She should be happy, not disappointed and achy.

He stretched an arm along the back of the sofa

with casual ease. "Will you be coming to my brother's campaign party this Sunday evening?"

So much for laid-back. Her master strategist ex had worked his timing well. Marianna hesitated, unsure of what to do with this confusing mix of charming and maneuvering.

Besides, facing his family had been tough enough last night, and that had been business. What would they think if she showed up for a social occasion? "I hadn't planned on it."

"It'll be a good promo opportunity for you professionally as well as a chance for us to show the world we can still be civil before we spill our secret."

He kept his body loose and lanky on the sofa, the perfect nonthreatening posture. It was a little too perfect, like he'd studied just such body language in a calculated bid to win his point.

"You're a good lawyer."

"I try."

She opted for honesty and let him do with it what he would. "What will your family say?"

"Absolutely nothing. They're all diplomats—comes from being politically inclined."

"True enough." She would be having far more contact with them than she'd expected because of the baby. "Through the whole divorce proceedings, your mother never said anything untoward to me."

"Lucky for you. More than once she demanded to know what I did wrong."

"Really?" That surprised her—and it didn't. Ginger adored her boys, but she'd never hesitated to call them on the carpet, even as adults. They all came by their driven natures honestly. "I'm sorry you caught flak. I hope she understands this is as much my fault as it is yours."

He stiffened, some of the studied ease of his body slid away. "You've never said that before."

"I'm sorry about that too then." She stared at his thoughtful breakfast offering. "I guess in spite of any attraction, we're just unsuited to live together. Our temperaments are too different."

He leaned forward, elbows on his knees, within touching distance. "I'm having a tough time remembering what all those differences are."

And right there blared the whopper difference beyond his workaholic tendencies. He'd never wanted to confront their issues, unbending in his insistence they didn't exist or would fade with time. Like how he wouldn't talk about Sophie while the wound of her loss festered to debilitating proportions.

Of course he would say she wanted to discuss things to death and pick at those sore spots. She stared at the jar of gourmet peanut butter in her white-knuckled grip. Eight months ago, she would have thrown it. Instead, she just wanted to cry over all they'd lost.

As much as she still found him infinitely desirable, she needed to steel herself to touch him without letting him seduce her back into his bed.

She lightly tucked her hand in his, still resting on his knee. "Sebastian, let's not ruin this momen—"

The door swung open and they both jolted back, the strength of Sebastian's fingers still imprinted on her senses. Ross filled the doorway, and for once, she resented his presence. She shot a wary glance at Sebastian. He sat calm as could be gathering up the food from the coffee table.

Ross lounged in the doorway tucking his hands in his jeans pockets, parting back his forest-green jacket. "Just wanted to check in and make sure you arrived all right."

"Sorry I was late." She scooped the antique auction catalog off the floor. "The evening meeting with Matthew and Ashley must have set my mental clock behind a bit."

"No problem." He strode deeper into her office space. "Working on the future senator's home is a top priority."

Sebastian shoved to his feet. "Thanks for your confidence in my brother's electability."

"You Landis men have a reputation of getting what you want."

Marianna tensed but Sebastian didn't snap back, and she actually found herself wanting to scowl at her boss.

Then Ross's easygoing smile returned. "I appreciate the overtime Marianna has been putting in lately. We're really excited about the company's expansion."

Sebastian's hands fisted by his sides. "What expansion?"

Oh, damn. She hadn't told him. Of course there hadn't been a need during the divorce proceedings as they were working to establish separate lives.

"Southern Designs is opening another branch upstate in Columbia. It is my hope that Marianna will be the acting manager and chief decorator."

Sprawled in a poolside chair, Sebastian tipped back a glass of seltzer water at his brother's campaign party, wishing for something stronger to drink but needing his wits around his tempting ex.

All this time he'd been concerned about Ross making a move on Marianna, and instead the guy had been working on flat-out moving her. Columbia wasn't at the end of the universe, but the three-hour distance stretched a helluva lot longer when he thought of the constraints it would put on his plans to be a daily presence in his child's life—and Marianna's. Would he even get any reassurance on that issue from her tonight?

Chamber music played lightly from a band off to one side under a lighted gazebo. The ocean breeze rippled across the pool scattered with magnolias and floating candles. His mother and Ashley had gone all out in planning this exclusive gathering at the Landis compound.

Invitations to their home were rare and coveted.

Ginger valued her privacy, however gathering political movers and shakers at her house would prove advantageous for Matthew. For the General and Ginger too, for that matter, as they entrenched themselves deeper and deeper into D.C. affairs of state.

He preferred his behind-the-scenes role of managing the family's fortune and taking on cases that spoke to his inner convictions. Marianna used to say she admired that about him.

And just that quickly, Sebastian felt it all the way to his bones the minute she walked out to the pool area. The sound of nearby conversations and polite laughter faded to zilch as that same tingling sensation he'd experienced throughout their marriage returned, even surprising him with its strength. Straightening in his chair, he saw her talking with his mother by a champagne fountain and a crystal bowl of iced shrimp.

God, he was glad she'd come. While he didn't begrudge his brother's happiness, listening to Matthew and Ashley make wedding plans wasn't always pleasant to do while in the middle of a divorce.

Marianna's wine-red dress hugged her body in quiet elegance, draping her curves from the high neckline down to midcalf. Tendrils of dark hair escaped the soft bundle of curls on top of her head, gently framing her face. When she turned to lift a canapé from a waiter's silver tray, Sebastian nearly choked on his drink.

The damn dress didn't have a back. Well, it did, but not much of one.

A single lock of hair trailed down her spine, brushing her pale skin as she tilted her head to listen to Ginger. Marianna's skin glowed with a translucent quality reminding him of the magnolias and candles floating in the pool.

"Hey, Mom, great party," Sebastian called as he grabbed his drink and strode closer to the women. "Hello, Marianna."

Setting his seltzer glass on the table behind her, with careful nonchalance, he traced a path down each vertebra, his callused finger snagging against her silky skin. Holy crap, was that silver glitter sprinkled along her shoulders?

"Good evening, Sebastian." She stepped away and crossed her arms over her breasts, shielding her response to his caress. "I was just asking your mother for the name of her caterer."

"And I was telling Marianna we're glad to have her here." His mother eyed the two of them with ill-disguised curiosity.

He wouldn't be able to dodge an interrogation much longer. His mother could be quietly relentless—the epitome of a steel magnolia.

And while he was on the subject of strong-willed women... When would Marianna want to tell the world about the baby? He preferred waiting until that announcement could be made along with their intent to get back together. He didn't want her settling too comfortably into the single-parent role.

He sure as hell didn't want her moving to Columbia.

Donning the perfect hostess smile, Ginger gestured across the patio. "There's Judge Johnson arriving with his new wife. I need to say hello. You two go enjoy yourselves." Ginger tossed the couple a wave as she located her husband and began the required social circulation.

Marianna faced him, the moon casting shadows through her long lashes. "I appreciate that you're willing to hold back on talking to your family. I know that can't be easy."

"They'll start pushing soon, but I'm a big boy. I'll talk when I'm ready."

"I know that firsthand."

Dangerous territory. She'd frequently complained about his reticence. Although she'd used stronger words—like stubborn jackass—to describe his refusal to discuss something before he'd had a chance to sort it out in his head. Growing up with talkative brothers, he'd found it easier to keep his own counsel and go his own way.

She crooked a finger and whispered, "I'll let you in on a secret, but you have to promise not to tell."

He brushed his finger just over her left breast. "Cross my heart."

Marianna pinched his wrist none too gently and moved his hand away. "That's not yours anymore."

As if he needed reminding of all he needed to win back. "What's the secret?"

"I'm really getting addicted to that gourmet peanut butter. Thank you."

"You're welcome." Sebastian leaned back, his arm resting behind her without touching. Checking out her body glitter and imagining how far it dusted beneath her dress proved plenty enjoyable for the moment. "You can uncross your arms now that Mom's gone."

"And you can pack away the flirting."

"As long as you're not packing your bags for Columbia."

"I was wondering how long it would take you to bring that up."

Matthew and Ashley burst onto the back porch, breaking the thread of tension. Sebastian retrieved his seltzer water for a much needed cooldown.

Ashley edged closer to the group. She was quiet but a surprisingly funny woman who Marianna had once mentioned she looked forward to calling sister. The bride-to-be filled a champagne flute from the fountain while Matthew slung an arm along Marianna's shoulder. "Is my brother behaving?"

"Sebastian's behavior has been borderline acceptable." Her smile tempered the words.

Sebastian tapped his glass against her arm. "Only borderline?"

She shivered as he lightly caressed the rim against

her bare skin. "I haven't shoved you in the pool yet, but it's going to be a near thing if you keep that up."

He pulled his glass back and drank from the spot that touched her. "There's an idea about the pool." Sebastian turned to his wide-eyed brother watching the two of them with ill-disguised confusion. "Matthew, you better watch your back because I'm thinking I owe you one for when you dunked me at that party Mom threw right after Marianna and I eloped—"

Ashley hooked arms with Matthew. "The photographers would love the chance to sell those pictures to the tabloids."

"Spoilsport," Sebastian mumbled. His soft-spoken future sister-in-law had an understated approach to getting her way, he would do well to study. Perhaps he needed to ease up on touching Marianna for the night. "So, Matthew, do you still have time in your campaign schedule for golfing next weekend?"

With some luck, Marianna would pick up on his mention of taking downtime, something she'd requested often enough in the past.

Matthew turned toward Ashley. "Do I?"

"Don't look at me. I'm not your boss."

Matthew snorted.

Ashley rolled her eyes. "Yes, Sebastian, Matthew may come out and play next Saturday."

Watching Matthew and Ashley, Marianna couldn't help but envy their ease together, their obvious love and compatibility. While she wouldn't begrudge them one moment, all that happiness and hope flat-out hurt right now.

But damn it all, she was tired of feeling sorry for herself. She was weary of grieving and crying. Her life wasn't perfect, but she had a helluva lot going for her right now. She had a baby to look forward to.

And a rekindled passion with her ex-husband.

Did she dare touch that fire again? They'd both been burned so badly. But, God, when had she become so timid?

It was after losing Sophie. The fight seemed to have gone out of her then. What a sad legacy to carry in the name of a precious little girl who'd brought so much joy.

Marianna stood taller and wondered how long she'd been slumping. Too long.

She didn't know where things were headed with Sebastian. Likely nowhere, although she imagined he had some honor-driven notion they should re-marry for the child. She disagreed. They'd taken off their wedding rings and turned the page on being married. Not even a relentless pursuit on his part could change that.

But in spite of any divorce decree, apparently they still had unfinished business between them— business they needed to sort through before the baby was born. Marianna took in the breadth of his shoulders, the slightly aloof tip of his head, her body already humming with awareness and an urge to explore the renewed attraction.

She was growing tired of his flirtatious strokes then pulling back. She was sexually frustrated and totally knew it. It was time Sebastian either quit the touching dance or own up to the fact that he wanted her, too.

Seven

Sebastian sprawled in a poolside chair for the bulk of the engagement party, making political chitchat as people strolled by. Mostly he used the spot as the perfect vantage point to watch Marianna while she helped his mother befriend wallflowers, give instructions to the waiters…

And open up the dance floor under the stars.

His body thrummed as he watched her sway to the music with his youngest brother, her laughter teasing his senses from across the patio. His decision to lay off touching her for a while was already playing with his sanity. Her smile tonight sliced right through the distance they'd put between them over the past months. Sebastian hadn't seen her happy like that in a long time. It must have something to do with that famed pregnancy glow.

A big band–era song struck up next and the General approached her. As Hank began to take her hand, his arms stopped in midair as he searched for a place covered by fabric. Sebastian stifled a smile.

Another hour passed until he watched Marianna sit alone for the first time, relaxing in a poolside chair. His no-touching decision was about to take a temporary hiatus. He deserved at least one dance, damn it. He strode over to her just as the strains of the final tune of the night played, a slower song as the band wound down.

"I think I'm the only man left who hasn't danced with you."

"You haven't asked me."

So she'd noticed his backing off. Good. At least he could gain some satisfaction from his restraint. Although right now, he wondered just how long that restraint would last.

He extended his hands. "May I have this dance? In the interest of being friends."

Marianna gulped as the full impact of Sebastian's appeal washed over her. The Southern gentleman to the hilt, he wore a navy jacket with his khakis in spite of the eighty-degree weather, a conservative maroon tie neatly knotted at his neck.

Odd thing, though, there were plenty of men

dressed much like him, equally attractive and powerful men, but none of *them* stirred her interest for even a second.

She placed her hands in Sebastian's, rising from the chair, stepping into the circle of his arms. His other palmed the bare skin low on her spine, his calluses calling to mind his strength. Marianna let him draw her near, his cheek just barely brushing her hair.

Slipping her fingers over his shoulder, she began to move her feet in rhythm with the music. Her breath twined with his in the sliver of air between them. He traced small, hypnotic patterns as he hummed along with the music.

Marianna's eyes drifted closed, and she let the attraction have its way with her senses, hot and steamy like the South Carolina heat. She leaned closer, her breasts heavy and full pressed against his chest. Their legs skimmed as their bodies mimicked a more fundamental dance, bringing back memories of better times.

She looked up at him, seeing all too clearly the desire in his eyes and becoming achingly aware of every inch of him. She knew that look well, and if they'd been anywhere else but in public, he would have her stripped down in seconds. As it was, she could only sway against him, hypnotized by the fierce want in his gaze, her whole body begging to be with him.

"Marianna, all flirting aside, you have to know

you're a beautiful, sexy woman," he whispered, his hands skimming tantalizing figure eights up and down her back.

Again, she felt the draw to take this window of time before the baby's birth to jump in and simply enjoy the urges her body demanded be filled. Even though Sebastian had given her space during the party, he didn't seem likely to tell her no.

He'd seemed calmer about her possible move than she'd expected, but she knew how well he could hide his steely streak. Maybe she needed to learn to trust her own strength of will in letting him know—calmly—where she stood. That sounded reasonable, especially for a woman with sensual longing supercharging through her veins.

She inclined her head just a hint, gazing at him for an electrified moment. "What do you think of a short-term arrangement as sex buddies?"

Sex buddies?

Stunned mute, Sebastian stared at Marianna in his arms on the starlit dance floor. She actually wanted to have sex with him. Now.

The rest of her words sunk in. She said something about a short-term arrangement, total BS in his mind, but he would deal with that later. He wasn't stupid enough to let this opportunity pass. "My place is more than a little crowded tonight. What do you say we go back to the house?"

She stared back at him with an unmistakable craving her eyes. "I say yes."

Restraining the urge to pump the air with his fist, Sebastian palmed her back and eyed the nearest exit. To hell with tossing around niceties on their way out, she seemed as determined as he was. Would they even make it to the house, or would they be pulling off the road again?

Five interminable minutes later, the valet had unearthed her car from the rows of guest vehicles. Sebastian snagged the keys and had the engine in Drive.

He eyed a convenient side road along the way but decided he wanted to take his time with her in the privacy of their house—in *his* bed. He could almost convince himself things were normal between them. Again?

Had they ever been normal? Their life together had started off at such a frenetic pace. They married three months after meeting. Marianna lost the baby on that hellish night in the mountains.

Then it was a breakneck pace through college and law school. The ups and downs of failed fertility treatments, and the adoption... He cut off thoughts that solved nothing. The past had no bearing on the present. He needed to forge ahead, build on what they had—the baby.

And a smoking-hot passion for each other that had ironically grown stronger during their divorce.

Sliding the car into Park outside their house, he lifted a stray lock of hair gracing her shoulder. "Have I told you how beautiful you look?"

"You mentioned it."

"Just checking."

"Sebastian."

"Yeah?"

"Shut up and kiss me."

"Yes, ma'am."

Urgency built with a need to roll free. He nibbled along her soft hand, vulnerable wrist, making short order of the trek up her arm to claim her mouth, hot, hard and fast. The familiar grip of desire that always simmered below the surface around Marianna roared to life.

He tangled a hand in her hair, combing through until her curls fell free, pins pinging along the gearshift. His other arm locked low around her waist and lifted her flush against him. Her soft curves fit against him, her hips rocking a promise he fully intended to accept.

"Inside," he whispered against her lips. "We've already done the sex-in-a-car deal. Let's take this to a bed."

"Yes," she gasped, her fingernails pressing through his jacket and into his shoulders with urgency, "but soon, please."

He reached to open his door while she held on to their kiss until the very…last…second. Sprinting around the hood of the car, he made it to her side just as she stepped out and back into his arms. Her feet tangled with his as they stumbled along the pavers.

She lost a shoe. He started to retrieve it, and she gripped his wrist, bringing his hand back to her waist as she kicked off the other high heel. "I'll get them later."

If Marianna didn't care about her precious shoes, she must mean business.

He scooped her off her bare feet and carried her up to the porch. Her fingers tunneled under his collar to tease his neck, her lips following suit while he fumbled with the keys.

Finally, the door swung open and he angled her into the cool hall. She slid down his body in a sensuous glide until she stood flush against him again. He booted the door closed and dodged Buddy zigzagging around them before curling up beside the door.

Sebastian backed her toward the stairs, his coat somehow falling off and landing on a Persian rug as he hit the first step. Damn, he adored her quick and efficient hands. And her eager mouth moving under his. Her soft breasts brushing against his chest.

Right now, he liked just about everything about her. She arched deeper into the kiss, her fingers making quick work of his tie, sending the strip of silk fluttering through the air.

Halfway up, he pinned her against the wall, needing to touch a lot more than they could with most of their clothes still on. His hands tunneled under her dress and up her legs while he kissed his way down her neck. Her head fell back against the wall with a thud as loud as her gasps of pleasure.

Sebastian caressed higher, along her hips then around to find she wore a skimpy thong. A possessive growl rumbled up and out as he thought about her dressed this way all evening long. He gripped her soft bare flesh and pressed her closer against him. Still not near enough to ease the throbbing in his pants—and not near enough for her either, if her urgent wriggles and breathy whimpers were anything to judge by.

Who the hell needed a bed anyway?

He slid a hand around front again, teasing along the edge of her thong, back and forth, just grazing her moist heat. The feel of her desire alone was almost enough to send him over the edge, but he held back. Wanting, aching to see her come apart before he gave in to his own driving need to be inside her.

"Sebastian," she gasped, hooking a long leg over his hip, "you're not playing fair. You promised we would hurry."

"Be patient." He blew lightly along her shoulder, some of her body glitter taking flight. "We'll get there."

He slid two fingers inside her panties for a firmer stroke followed by a slow dip inside her. Then out. Repeating again and again while imagining just how good the sweet moist clamp of her would feel around more than just his fingers.

Her other knee buckled, and he anchored her against the wall. She gasped as fast as his heart pounded inside his chest, each breath faster as he could see her nearing completion. She rocked against his touch while slipping her hand to his belt buckle and damn but she already had him buzzing…

Except wait—that was his cell phone, clipped to his waistband, set on vibrate.

"Ignore it." He circled his passion-slicked fingers around her tight bud of nerves.

"Probably just work trying to intrude on our love life for the four hundredth time."

"Work can go to hell tonight," he grumbled between tight teeth.

His BlackBerry buzzed. He pitched it to the floor and kissed her quiet, his tongue stroking the inside of her mouth as thoroughly as his fingers playing lower. The cell phone buzzed again.

Marianna nipped along his lower lip. "Maybe we should just check the caller ID."

"Not so inclined right now."

She reached to tip the phone's LCD screen upward and instantly stilled in his arms, her foot sliding back to the stairway. "Sebastian, it's the General. What if it's a family emergency?"

As much as he wanted to think she was overreacting, he couldn't ignore the fact that the General never called late. Ever.

Sebastian grabbed the phone just as it stopped ringing, then hit Redial. He picked up after one ring.

"General? Sebastian here. What's up?" Besides him.

"You know I wouldn't bother you this late if it wasn't important, but your mother needs you. Kyle's plane has been shot down in Afghanistan." The nightmarish words feared by every family with a military relative echoed through the airwaves. "They don't know if he survived the crash."

Marianna pressed a hand to the dashboard, her brain struggling to change gears as quickly as Sebastian shifting into fourth on her car as he raced back to the Landis compound. There'd been no discussion of leaving her at home. Kyle had been a part of her family for nine years. Just thinking of Sebastian's lighthearted brother possibly lying out there somewhere dead...

She wanted to be with the family. She *needed* to be there, could only imagine how terrified his mother must be. Her own heart ached so deeply over losing Sophie, yet she had the reassurance that her daughter was still alive. What kind of hell it would be to fear for your child's life?

And Sebastian... Yes, she had to be there for him, even though he would never ask, much less acknowledge he had needs. What must be churning inside him right now? His jaw flexed in what had to be a teeth-grinding clench as he powered down the four-lane road. His fist stayed tight around the gearshift. In spite of the muscles bulging beneath his shirtsleeves, he held steady at the speed limit.

Just barely.

Maybe if she could get him to talk. "What else did the General have to say?"

"Only that Kyle was working some kind of covert operation with the Air Force's Office of Special Investigations. The transport plane that was carrying him went off radar. Radio transmissions indicate they were shot down. They're searching for the wreckage now."

"God, Sebastian, I'm so sorry. Your mother must be frantic."

"I'm not borrowing trouble. Kyle's tough. He's a survivor."

He was also just the reckless, selfless kind to die saving everyone else. But that didn't need to be said. Sebastian knew his own brother well enough.

"Anything else?" she asked, more to keep him talking than out of any expectation to discover more.

He shook his head. "The media hasn't gotten hold of the story yet. The Air Force is trying to keep Kyle's name out of the news in case he's evading."

She shuddered at the possibility of him in the hands of enemies. If they realized they had the son of a politically influential family in their grasp… The horrendous possibilities were unthinkable.

Sebastian stopped for a red light, revving the engine as if willing the miles between them and the compound to go by all the faster. The light turned green and he accelerated.

Headlights blinded her through her window. Brakes squealed. Her muscles tensed in anticipation of the likely crash. She braced her hand more firmly against the dash, her other arm hugging her waist, her baby, with a fierce maternal drive to protect—

Cursing, Sebastian twisted the steering wheel, jolting the car. Her body flung to the right, rapping her head against the passenger window with a painful snap.

Then everything went dark.

Eight

Sebastian paced in the emergency room waiting area, still not certain if Marianna and their baby were all right.

Damn it, why had he let himself become distracted while driving? Sure he managed to avoid the other vehicle—barely. The drunk driver had embedded his car in a telephone pole, then staggered around without so much as a scratch. Marianna, however, had been knocked unconscious.

The present resembled the past too closely for him to shrug it off. Again, he was in an E.R. waiting to hear if Marianna and their baby were all right. Even thoughts of the ride itself made him break out in a cold sweat. As with nine years ago, he'd driven like a bat out of hell with Marianna in the car. He was lucky he hadn't killed her then. But what about now?

He still didn't know because the doctor had banished him from the room out into this damn small space where he kept knocking his legs on metal furniture every time he turned around. And the noises, God, they jangled in his ears. The older lady two gurneys down the hall who kept up a steady stream of complaints whenever a nurse walked by. A teenager crying quietly as she spoke into a cell phone. The occasional drum of the EMTs' feet as they raced in with a new patient.

How much longer would he have to cool his heels? He kicked an end table aside, which drew his attention to his shoes, the ones Marianna had given him for Christmas. Shoes that would have been beside her bed if this night had gone differently.

He couldn't even wrap his brain around what might be going on with his brother. Somebody needed to cough up good news. Soon.

The sliding doors swished open to admit more of the late-night crowd, except a much-better dressed new batch—his family. They must not have had time to change out of their party clothes before the call about Kyle came in. His mother rushed toward him, Matthew and Ashley close on her heels.

He bolted forward and slid an arm around his

mother's shoulders. "Have you heard anything about Kyle?"

Matthew shook his head. "Nothing yet. The General's out in the parking lot making more calls, trying to tap into his military contacts. Jonah stayed at the house to man the phones."

Sebastian exhaled hard, wishing for more information while grateful that at least there hadn't been bad news. Still, his mother must be feeling torn in two tonight. Her clothes might be camera-ready perfect, but the rubber gardening clogs on her feet declared how frazzled she must have been as she rushed out the door.

"Mom, you didn't need to come here." He gave her a light one-armed hug. "You've got enough to worry about right now."

"You're my son, too." She pressed a maternal kiss to his cheek, the strain around her eyes painfully evident. "Every child is equally important in my heart."

"I'm okay. It's Marianna—" and their baby "—that I'm concerned about."

She gripped his arm, her eyes searching his face. "You said on the phone that you were with Marianna, but you didn't say what happened to her."

"She's still in the exam room." He scrubbed a hand over his face. "She hit her head on the passenger window when I swerved to miss a drunk driver."

"Son, I can't even begin to understand what's

going on between the two of you lately. I'm just glad you're both all right."

Half the time *he* didn't even know where things stood between him and his ex-wife. "Thank you for coming, but you really can go home. I've got this."

She cupped his cheek. "You of all my boys understand the fears of a parent's heart."

For a second he thought she'd found out about the baby, then he realized she meant Sophie. He stood stock-still, frozen from the inside out. No one other than Marianna had dared mention his daughter's name around him, not after he'd cut off conversations often enough. That his mother would bring her up now only proved how stressed she must be. He stayed silent and let his mother keep talking.

"Even though you know Sophie's well cared for, it's difficult not to worry about our children when they're out of our sight, much less when you know you can't see them again. You and Marianna have been through so much these past months."

Now that part, he had heard from his mother— her softly spoken suggestion that he and Marianna not go through with the divorce so quickly. Which only proved how well he and Marianna had hidden their problems from even those closest to them. The lead up to ending their marriage had been protracted and painful, dragging out over the past two years.

"Sebastian, did you hear what I said?" his

mother's worried voice yanked him back into the cold, antiseptic present.

"Sure, Mom, absolutely." He hoped he hadn't just agreed to something too outrageous.

Matthew took her elbow, angling her toward the exit. "You've seen with your own eyes that he's okay. Let's go back to the house."

The doors leading to the exam rooms swished open and Sebastian pivoted fast, his family pretty much fading away. Dr. Cohen strode through with brisk efficiency, her red glasses hanging from her neck. "Mr. Landis, Marianna is awake. By all indications, she and the baby are both perfectly fine."

He gripped the back of a chair, his legs suddenly not too steady under him. "How much longer until I can go back to see her?"

"In a few minutes. She's getting dressed, then you can take her home. She'll need someone to check on her through the night, just to be on the safe side with that bump on her head." The doctor tapped his arm with the edge of the chart. "You've got a tough one there, both her and the baby."

"Thank you again, Dr. Cohen. I appreciate your coming to the hospital so quickly." The E.R. docs had said they could handle Marianna's case. But with the nightmare of that long-ago miscarriage still so starkly fresh in his mind, he'd demanded they call Marianna's ob-gyn to check her over.

The doors slid closed after Dr. Cohen, and he

turned around to find his family gawking wide-eyed back at him. Even the General had arrived just in time to hear everything, his arm already around Ginger to steady her. Ah, crap. Wrapped up in his need for news about Marianna's condition, he'd all but forgotten his relatives were even there.

"Baby?" his mother whispered, her smile quivering in time with a tear.

So much for waiting to tell everyone about the pregnancy. At least Marianna wouldn't be able to blame him for spilling the news.

Matthew scratched his head, cheeks puffing with a long, slow exhale. "That sure answers a lot of questions, like why you two have been so chummy all of the sudden."

Sebastian rocked back on his heels. "That day she fainted at the courthouse, we found out about the pregnancy when she saw the doctor afterward." He figured it wasn't any of his family's business that Marianna actually had known a few hours *before* the divorce, a fact that still grated. "Marianna and I wanted to find the right time to tell you—once we've had a chance to make plans."

His brother clapped him on the shoulder. "Congratulations, bro."

His mother rushed to hug him. "I'm happy for both of you. A baby is always cause for joy."

All the emotionalism started to make him itchy. He just wanted to see Marianna—and holy crap—there was still the uncertainty with his brother. How could he have forgotten about Kyle for even a second? "About Kyle, Marianna and I will be over as soon as—"

His mother held up a hand. "You need to be with Marianna, and it sounds like she should rest. We'll keep you posted the second we hear anything."

He hesitated, his need for news about his brother at odds with concerns for Marianna. "You're sure?"

"There's nothing any of us can do now except wait." She nodded toward the door leading back to the exam rooms. "Go be with Marianna."

His mother was right. He couldn't help Kyle, but he could take care of Marianna. "We'll be by tomorrow to talk more."

And once his mother didn't have so much worrying her, he intended to make it clear Marianna would be a part of their family in every possible way. He would get his life on track.

He couldn't get Sophie back. But he damn well wasn't going to let anyone take a child of his away again, not even his stubborn ex-wife.

Marianna rested her forehead against the cool glass of the car window and looked out at the homes in their neighborhood. *Her* neighborhood, since Sebastian had moved out.

Had it really only been a couple of hours since she and Sebastian had raced into the house expecting to be sex buddies? Now they didn't know if

Kyle was alive or dead. They themselves could have died because of that drunk driver.

Life had a way of reshuffling cards faster than she could think. Like with her teen pregnancy and how her elderly parents had been so disappointed in her. Would things have turned out differently— better—for her and for Sebastian if she'd pushed him for more time to get to know each other rather than rushing into marriage?

As he pulled into their driveway, she slid her hand over her stomach and her eyes toward him. The two most important people in her world were okay. She should take great comfort in that, yet she still felt so unsettled. Yes, Sebastian mattered to her and in a way that went beyond sex buddies. But what had changed between them? Feelings weren't so easily cut off simply because they'd signed their names to a divorce decree.

None of which she could deal with or resolve tonight, not with the fear of that near-wreck leaving her emotions raw. And certainly not while concerns for his brother loomed.

Sebastian opened his door and met her as she swung her legs out. She couldn't help but compare this somber walk along the pavers with their frantic rush up the porch steps earlier. Her senses hummed with the memory of his arms wrapped around her, carrying her inside. She could use the comfort of his embrace again.

What if he wanted to pick up where they'd left

off on the stairway earlier? She wasn't sure if that was wise or not, but she did know she needed to be honest with him.

She stepped inside, kneeling to catch Buddy before he sprinted outside. She glanced up at Sebastian as he secured the front door. "I don't know if we should have sex tonight."

He pocketed the keys, studying her with inscrutable eyes. "You need to rest. I'll wake you every couple of hours."

He'd given in so easily that she didn't know whether to be relieved or insulted. "I'm sorry to keep you from your family. You must be worried sick about Kyle. *I'm* worried sick about him."

He reached down to pat Buddy, calming him with the slow, steady dog-whisperer way of his. "There's nothing I can do for Kyle, and Matthew promised to call if there's any news." Buddy circled them once more then trotted away, nails clicking on the hardwood floors before she heard the doggie door swish open and closed. "I'm where I'm supposed to be right now. You and this baby are my family."

The sincerity of his words whispered over her like a breeze stirring the water at night, disrupting and enticing all at once. "The baby's fine. You can stop worrying about that much, at least."

His jaw flexed as hard as the muscles bulging along sleeves of his jacket. "I shouldn't have let the news about my brother compromise your safety."

He blamed himself? That was so unfair—and such an awful burden to carry. "Good God, Sebastian, it wasn't your fault. The other guy was drunk."

He gripped her shoulders, his face tight with unmistakable pain. "I thought you were going to die tonight."

His words now echoed words he'd spoken nine years ago after she'd woken from surgery after the ectopic pregnancy had ruptured her fallopian tube. Suddenly she realized the hell he must have gone through tonight, experiencing what must have seemed like a replay of the past. Could he somehow have blamed himself for that night as well?

Damn keeping her distance.

Her hand gravitated up to caress his neck, her thumb stroking his tensed jaw. "Sebastian..."

She didn't even know what else to say to him. Then his mouth sealed over hers with a fierceness that touched her heart and rekindled her banked yearning from earlier. Each tender stroke of his hands over her shoulders nudged aside the emotional boundaries she'd tried to put in place with him. His one admission of fear for her made her more weak-kneed than the velvet sweep of his tongue.

Sebastian slipped a hand behind her head and cupped her neck. With the other, he palmed her waist, his fingers hot along her back exposed by the party dress she'd chosen hours ago. Marianna slid her hand inside his jacket, her fingers spreading wide against his chest, digging past his shirt.

He guided her face to his, flicking his tongue along the seam of her full mouth. She opened, begging for more, needing the reassurance of connecting on any level, even if just the physical. With a whispery moan, Marianna slid her arms around Sebastian's neck, deepening their kiss. Their mouths mated with the familiar, yet unexplainable frenzy she'd come to accept as inevitable.

His hand crept up, cupping the curve of her breast, his calluses rasping against the silky fabric as he caressed the added fullness brought on by pregnancy. The tightening bud of response echoed a thread of longing pulling tauter inside her.

Sebastian paused, his mouth hovering a scant breath away. "Are you all right, with the baby—"

"I'm fine." Marianna plucked at the buttons down his shirt. "The doctor said so. In fact, it's a good thing for me to stay awake. Remember?"

"Let me know if—"

"I will," she said between kisses as they started up the stairs, trailing clothes behind them, his jacket, their shoes, the undressing going faster this go-round.

As the stairs turned, he stopped on the landing, pressing her to the wall again. She didn't want to think about tomorrow or their failed past. She wanted to dive into this craving for Sebastian and never climb back out. Apparently, his feelings weren't too different from hers because he kissed her with a fierce passion that had her legs going weak while her arms conversely grew stronger as she held on.

A white flutter snagged her attention as Sebastian tossed his shirt down the stairs. When had he peeled it off? She didn't care as long as her hands got to explore more of him.

Her dress slid down her shoulders, and she couldn't recall how it got there. Again, not that she cared as long as he swept it aside and away...ah, yes. She pressed her near-naked body to his.

He bracketed her with his arms, his hands flat on either side of the wall. Sebastian leaned forward, his breath steaming over her skin, sending shivers down her spine, making her all the more aware of the chair railing at her back.

His lips crashed down on hers again. She met his power, gripping his hair to bring him closer. Her mouth opened, wide and hungry as she tangled her tongue with his in a battle of wills that promised much for both of them if neither gave up.

That last flight of stairs looked like a never ending trek. Marianna sagged, her arms locked around his neck and his arm hooked around her back, the only restraints keeping her from sliding to the...

The floor. Yes, the floor of the landing was perfect and immediate, taking away those last few steps that would give her time to reason her way out of something she wanted, needed so damn much.

Sebastian eased her to the thick wool rug on the landing. "Now? Here?"

"Absolutely."

She rocked her hips against his, moaning at the

glorious sensation of being intimately close to him again. His leg wrapped around hers, bringing her nearer, nestling her against the throbbing length of him. He slipped a restless hand inside her bra. His thumb caressed tantalizing circles over her swollen breasts. She arched her back to fill his palm, the increased pressure only making her crave more. More of this. More of him.

He growled low and hot against her ear. "I thought you didn't want to have sex."

"I don't." The real reasoning for her words earlier flowered in her mind. "I want us to *make love* again."

And yes, she wanted that even as she knew it could well be impossible for them to recapture.

She saw his eyes shift, the blue cooling to that shade that meant he was working to distance himself from deeper emotions. Emotions he'd called wasted drama in the months leading up to their divorce. If she let him think too long now, they would lose what little chance they had to connect on any level tonight.

"Hurry." Marianna worried her bottom lip between her teeth as she struggled with his belt. She freed him with a caress too slow to be anything other than deliberate. Sebastian throbbed in her hand as his fingers skimmed aside her bra and panties.

He propped on his elbows to keep the bulk of his weight off her, his gaze sweeping down her body with an admiration a woman would have to be comatose not to enjoy.

Comatose. Just the word brought that fearful moment in the car, those frightening seconds when she'd woken up in the hospital. All of it reminding her of what she could have lost tonight.

Making her determined not to take whatever she could.

She guided him inside her, carefully, slowly, then slid her hands inside his pants to urge him deeper.

He pulled his mouth from hers. "Look at me."

Her lashes fluttered, but didn't open. She guided his face closer, bowed up to meet him.

He inched away, tightening his grip on her hair, her curls draping down a step. "Marianna, look at me."

She nuzzled his neck before staring up into his eyes, half afraid of what she would find. "Okay. I'm looking."

He tipped her face, his pupils so wide with an intensity that pushed the blue to a thin ring. He thrust into her. "My name."

"What?" What was he talking about, and how he could even think, much less talk?

He stroked again, his hand grazing over her hair as it trailed down the wooden stairs. "Say *my* name."

She pressed her lips to his, refusing to let jealousy ruin this moment. "Sebastian." She raked her fingers along his shoulders. "Sebastian."

Marianna circled her hips against him, willing

him to toss aside some of his seemingly endless supply of control. So damn frustrating when any semblance of control seeped from her the minute he touched her with his hands, his eyes, even his words. She closed her eyes, locked together by something stronger than she even wanted to fight anymore. She simply let their need with its own special frenetic rhythm have its way, driving her closer to completion with each thrust of his body.

Release exploded through her and she repeated his name arching her back until her toes curled. With a hoarse shout, he knotted his fingers in her hair and shuddered against her until finally he dropped to his side and pulled her to him.

Their bodies bound by sweat, tangled legs and a strange bond she couldn't shake free, she knew traveling up that last flight of stairs was the least of their worries.

Nine

Sebastian lay in his own bed again for the first time in eight months. Wide awake. Not that he could have slept even if he didn't need to wake up Marianna every two hours.

Waiting for the phone to ring with news about his brother was hell.

He'd tried to distract himself by going downstairs and logging on to Marianna's computer. He'd accessed his bank account, looking into different kinds of trust funds to set up for the baby. And sure, he'd spent much of that time trying to figure out a way he could persuade Marianna to quit her job and take things easy. Was it so wrong of him to want to care for her, especially on a night like this that brought to the fore how damn fragile life could be?

The gauzy stuff that twisted around the canopy railing swished with the gusts from the ceiling fan. They no doubt needed the cooling relief after their workout on the landing and again in bed.

He twined a lock of her hair around a finger, careful not to twist too tightly and risk waking her early. He checked the clock. 4:25 a.m. Another five minutes to go, and he didn't intend to rouse her a second before.

He studied her face and how the soft puffs of breath between her lips feathered the strand of hair draped across her cheek. After so long apart, he welcomed the opportunity to look his fill. A pale shoulder peeked from beneath the sheet draping along her curves, and he resisted the urge to sweep it away.

What the hell had happened between them on the way to the bedroom? He'd wanted sex, along with a forgetfulness he'd always been able to find in her body in the past.

Their coming together had been anything but peaceful. She'd pinned him with her eyes, held him in some kind of intense moment that stoked his craving for her even as it made him want to back the hell away. She needed something more from him—she always had.

He would just have to keep her distracted with what they did well long enough for her to forget the parts they seemed destined to mess up. He glanced at the clock.

4:30 a.m. on the dot.

Sebastian peeled away the Egyptian cotton sheet inch by inch, kissing every revealed patch of her—her breasts, her stomach, her hips—until she wriggled beneath him. Marianna stretched with a feline grace that almost had him sliding inside her again. Almost. He needed more time to haul his defenses into place around her before she ambushed him with another "make love" line.

He looked up the length of her body, his hand grazing down to tease behind her knee. "Are you awake?"

"I am now." She smiled back at him with heavy-lidded arousal.

He brought his hand up and in front of her face. "How many fingers?"

"Three."

"Perfect."

She lightly stroked his jaw. "Has there been any word about Kyle?"

He turned to kiss her palm. "Nothing yet, but I'm going with the no news is good news philosophy." Wanting distraction from a subject that frustrated him with how little he could do, he turned his attention to something he could fix. "How about a snack before morning sickness has a chance to kick in?"

Marianna studied him with concerned eyes for

a second beyond his comfort level before she gave him the smile he needed.

"You're a man after my own heart." She sat up, clutching the blue-and-yellow-striped sheet to her chest. "I'm craving some of that raspberry chocolate peanut butter in the fiercest way."

There she went with the heart talk again. He tamped down the twinge of unease and swung his feet off the bed. He retrieved his boxers while she wrapped the sheet around her body, toga style.

She grinned over her shoulder. "Last one to the kitchen has to feed the other one while naked."

"Sounds like a win-win situation to me," he called after her as she raced ahead of him.

He took his time following her, already looking forward to the pleasure of bringing food to her lips and watching near-ecstasy spread across her face. Even the computer room with its glowing screen couldn't compete with what Marianna had to offer right now.

Once in the kitchen, he clicked on a single band of track lighting, illuminating the state-of-the-art cooking space. She'd taken the most time decorating here, a place to indulge her culinary prowess. Memories ambushed him.

Of her excitement over picking out the mammoth cooktop.

Of her on a ladder hanging pots from the rack attached to the ceiling.

Of their newborn daughter snoozing in a baby

seat on the floor beside the table, Marianna rocking the tiny chair with her foot while chopping vegetables on the island.

Definitely different from his late-night snack in the dark office kitchenette. "Have a seat and prepare to be fed."

She perched on a bar stool at the tiled island while he opened the stainless steel refrigerator. How long had it been since they'd indulged in a post-sex snack? He honestly couldn't remember when. Any lightheartedness had left their relationship a long time ago.

He wondered now how he'd let that happen when Marianna's uninhibited laugh was one of the things he enjoyed most about her. He could use some of her brightness tonight with the past dogging his heels and concern for Kyle kicking in his gut.

Sebastian snagged a bottle of sparkling water and set it on the kitchen island by the fruit basket. He checked the pantry, and yes, she'd stored all the gourmet peanut butters there, in a line, in front of anything else on the shelf. Each one had been opened for more than just a sample.

He passed her the chocolate raspberry, then pulled a knife from the block. He sliced an apple and handed a piece to her. "What is it about peanut butter that calls to a person regardless of income level?"

She scooped it through the gourmet mix. "Must be something to do with tapping into memories from when we were little."

More so than she could have realized. Damn. It was one helluva a time to dredge up childhood memories. But talking about Kyle was a lot easier than even thinking about Sophie, especially since he *had* to believe that his brother was fine.

His knife slowed along the apple. "Kyle and I used to eat peanut butter and marshmallow sandwiches when we were kids."

She looked up, surprise widening her eyes before a sheen of tears hovered on her lids. "You two have always been close."

"More so when we were younger, before we got caught up in our careers."

He paused, waiting for the snappy comeback about him putting his job above everything else. But for once, she didn't take the shot. His shoulders relaxed, and he hadn't realized until that moment he'd even tensed them.

"This one time when we were about nine and ten, we spent most of the summer playing in a forest behind our house. Well, it seemed like a forest, anyway. It was probably just a few trees with a walking path."

He sliced piece after piece from the apple until only the core remained. "We hung out there all day long. We'd pack peanut butter and marshmallow sandwiches, take a gallon jug of Kool-Aid. And we dug tunnels."

"Tunnels?" She leaned forward on her elbows, intent and ever elegant even in a sheet.

"We dug deep trenches, laid plywood over the top, then piled a layer of dirt over that." The fun of those times wrapped around him again. "We were lucky we didn't die crawling around in there. We could have suffocated. Or our whole roofing could have given way if someone had unknowingly stepped on one of those boards."

"What did your mother say?"

"She never knew." No doubt she would have grounded both of them for all of eternity, and they'd deserved it. They were too fearless as kids. Kyle was still too damn reckless for his own good. "We made Jonah stand guard and let us know if she was coming."

"What did you have to pay him to get him to go along with that?"

"Who said we paid him?" Chuckling, he pitched the apple core in the trash. "He's the youngest. He did what we said."

Her gentle smile warmed her eyes and the room. "And Matthew?"

"He's too much of a rule follower. We never let him in on the secret." He tried to make light of the memory, but still, it sucked him under. "Kyle was especially into it. I should have known then he would go into the military."

Marianna slid off the bar stool and slipped her

arms around his waist, resting her head on his bare chest. Concern for his brother damn near choked him, but no way in hell was he going to let it cripple him. Especially not in front of Marianna.

He glided his hands up and down her back, trying to keep himself in check when he wanted nothing more than to try and recapture some of that forgetfulness she offered. She tipped her head up to press a kiss against his neck, her arms clenching tighter around him. The lump in his throat grew larger. He had to do something and do it fast, or she would cut him right open.

Sealing his mouth to hers before she could blindside him by saying something sympathetic, Sebastian cupped her bottom and lifted her against him. Pleasing her would most definitely please him.

Marianna wanted to sink back into their old habit of losing themselves in sex. Falling into an old pattern was so much easier than forging a new one. His story about playing with Kyle still twisted her already vulnerable heart.

His hands low on her buttocks, he lifted her, setting her onto the island. The sheet slithered from her shoulders to pool around her hips in a cool glide against rapidly heating flesh. The silence of their house swelled around them, reminding her of how lonely the past months had been.

"Hey there, you," Marianna said, more to chase away the silence than to talk. "You lost the race to the kitchen. You were supposed to feed me while naked."

"So take them off," he whispered against her ear.

She thumbed along the waistband of his boxers with a snap, then sketched her hands up to his defined pecs, honed from hours on the water and golf course. She brushed her cheek across the sprinkling of bristly hair on his chest, kissing and blowing dry paths down to his stomach and back up again with teasing restraint.

Staring straight into his heavy-lidded eyes, she teased along the elastic in his boxers again. She hooked her thumbs in his waistband, scratching a light trail over his hips until the underwear slipped down his legs. His low growl of appreciation urged her to continue.

He kicked the boxers aside, molding their bodies flush against each other. Marianna couldn't contain her moan of pleasure at the sensation of skin against skin.

Sebastian pressed his forehead to hers. "You can't know how good you feel."

She slid her hands along his five o'clock shadow and up to cradle his face. "I think I do because it's probably much the same as how you feel against me."

He sealed his mouth to hers and nudged her knees apart. He stepped closer, the throbbing length of his arousal pressing against her slick core. She wriggled, sending sparks through her, showering faster than she would have expected after the pleasure he'd already brought her tonight.

His hand trailed lower, dipped, teasing the bundled center of nerves, launching her over the first threshold too soon, too fast, scaring her a little with how much power he held over her responses. She couldn't imagine being with anyone else, which left only the option of working things out with Sebastian—or being alone for the rest of her life.

Then a second wave of pleasure ripped through her, stealing her ability to think, to doubt. Tremors shook through her, convulsing her fingers around the hot length of him tearing mingling groans from them both.

Settling himself more firmly against her, Sebastian slid inside with a tantalizing slowness. Deeper, he filled her. Her eyes drifted closed and she arched her back, feeling her body stretch with a pleasurable ache as she accommodated him. Hooking her ankles behind his waist, she savored being joined with him again, having as much of him as she wanted tonight.

And tomorrow? She couldn't let the chilling thought encroach on what she felt right now. And she did feel so much.

When he didn't move, Marianna looked up into his face. She wished she hadn't. Sebastian's blue eyes sparked familiar intensity that unsettled her all the way down to her painted toenails. He hadn't changed any more than she had, and foolishly, she still wanted him.

Marianna buried her face in his neck and rocked her hips until he joined in the rhythm. Relentlessly, he drove her to the brink and then slowed. Taking her there again, he hurtled her over with a force that ripped cries of release just before he followed her into the explosion of sensation.

She sagged limply against him, gasping for breath, losing track of how long they stayed locked that way before he gathered her into his arms. Marianna relaxed against his chest all the way up the stairs and into the bedroom they'd once shared.

He placed her on the bed again gently. His back to her, he set the alarm clock. For work?

Then she remembered the bump on her head and the doctor's orders to wake her up every two hours. The car wreck seemed like days ago, so much had happened in such a short time. She hadn't thought of the tender spot on her scalp since coming home.

Marianna stared at the gossamer shadows flickering across her bedroom ceiling as the moonlight filtered through her lacy canopy. The cloudy shadows danced across the spackling, shifting, merging, changing, just like her turbulent life. Turning her head on the pillow, she gazed at the cause of her turmoil sleeping beside her.

She couldn't escape the niggling doubts grabbing

hold in her mind, threatening what little ground she and Sebastian had found here tonight. When he'd carried her up to the bedroom again, she'd seen the computer screen glowing and knew she hadn't left it on. She didn't have to ask if he'd been working.

Marianna pressed a hand to her stomach, visualizing her—their—child. She wanted this baby, needed him or her. She just wasn't sure how to handle the father, this complex man who evoked tantalizing whispers of emotions she'd thought were lost to her.

The ringing telephone jarred Marianna awake. Reality blazed through her as brightly as the early morning sunlight slanting through the blinds.

The phone rang again. With information about Kyle?

She reached beside her to shake Sebastian awake. Her hand smacked through empty space before thumping the mattress. Where was he? Back at work on the computer again?

She rolled to grab the phone just as the ringing stopped. The light on the handset showed another receiver was in the use somewhere else, the caller ID confirming the call had come from his mother's house.

Sebastian wasn't gone. Relief seeped through her even as she worried about Kyle. She scraped away the covers and snatched her silk robe from the closet. Whichever way the conversation went, she needed to be with Sebastian when he heard the news.

She yanked the tie closed around her waist and started down the hall toward the stairs. The near-by sound of Sebastian's voice slowed her feet. She turned to follow the sound, not far, coming from…

Sophie's old bedroom.

Her stomach clenched tight at the thought of his stepping into that room of tiny roses, ruffles and memories. Had he simply gone in there because it was closest when the phone rang? That had to be the case, because Lord knew he had never set foot over that threshold since the day Sophie left their lives.

She paused in the open doorway, her bare toes curling on the cool hardwood floor. She studied his profile as he sat in the rocking chair where they'd both wiled away nights soothing Sophie back to sleep.

"Uh-huh…" Sebastian spoke into the receiver. "That's great news, General. And when will Kyle be able to call?"

She sagged against the door frame in relief. His brother must be fine. Thank God. She kept her eyes on Sebastian, not yet ready to look around the space she'd decorated with love and hope. Still every detail of the vintage cabbage rose nursery stayed in her mind from the glistening cherry wood furniture to the yellow and pink patterns.

Even Sophie's sweet scent remained in her memory long past when it faded from the room— baby detergent mingled with mild soap. She swallowed down a lump swelling from her chest to her throat and focused on Sebastian.

His head nodded in time with whatever the General was saying. "Thanks for calling. Make sure Mom tells him I'm glad those trench digging skills of his worked out so well."

A half smile tugged at his face in spite of the weary hunch of his shoulders.

"Good night then—uh, or rather, good morning." He disconnected the phone, his hands falling to his knees, his head thudding back against the rocker.

She almost rushed in to comfort him, but she recalled how he'd frozen in the kitchen when she'd hugged him. Then he'd shifted quickly to sex as a distraction—not that she could blame him when she'd been a willing participant.

Somehow, even sex had seemed better than a total rejection, another reaction she'd experienced often enough right after Sophie was taken. She could already see the way it would play out. He would straighten back into big strong man mode, impervious to silly things like emotions or pain.

So she would let him have his private moment to deal with whatever was going on inside that mind of his. Marianna backed a step away as Sebastian turned his head toward her.

"Don't go," he said.

For once his face stayed open, no walls in sight. Just an intense and slightly weary man, and yet somehow he looked stronger than ever to her. Had something shifted between them in the kitchen after all? Could everything she'd begun feeling again be flowing both ways?

She hovered in the doorway warily. "I didn't realize you knew I was here."

"I always know when you walk into a room."

Now wasn't that a nerve sizzling notion?

She eased deeper inside until her feet padded along the soft give of the pink and yellow braid rug. "I take it from what you said on the phone that all is well with Kyle."

"Yes, not even a scratch on him," he confirmed. "Apparently someone lurking around on a mountain shot down the plane. Everyone survived the crash landing, but they'd abandoned the site to hide out from rebels. So the rescue mission took a while longer."

"Those hours must have been horrifyingly long for your brother."

"I don't even want to think about it."

Of course he didn't. Sebastian was all about closing down the past and moving ahead as if it never happened. She trailed her fingers along the large armoire, door open with Sophie's baptismal gown on display. With the ache so fresh again in this room, she actually wanted some of Sebastian's selective amnesia.

He pointed toward the bags filling the crib. "I see you went shopping for the baby."

She looked at those sacks full of all things pink and thought of the tears that went into that recent shopping trip. Forgetting be damned. She just couldn't hold back any longer. If he truly wanted to try at some kind of renewed connection between them, he would have to accept who she was and how she dealt with life. He would have to learn how to change.

Her hand leaving the silky baptismal dress, she turned to Sebastian, letting all the grief flow freely through her, and asked, "Do you ever think about her?"

Ten

Do you ever think about her?

Marianna's question burned through Sebastian's ears to sear his insides. He didn't need to ask who Marianna meant. Just the hint of Sophie seemed to bring her back into the nursery so tangibly he could have sworn her heard his daughter cooing from the crib. He forced his grip to loosen on the arms of the rocker before his fingers went numb.

The instinct to end the conversation pounded through him. But only momentarily. If he ever wanted to make things right with Marianna, he couldn't keep repeating the same mistakes. He needed to accept that Sophie—and his unwillingness to share the grief with his wife—dug half the chasm in their marriage.

"I think about Sophie all the time." The words grated all the way up his throat.

Even as he'd tried to forget her, tried not to even think her name, still he found himself wondering if she was fed, held, warm enough, cool enough. Loved enough.

Marianna stopped in front of the crib, her hands gripping the lowered railing that would never be raised again for their daughter. "Her first birthday is at the end of this week."

"I remember."

She reached into one of the shopping sacks and pulled out a tiny pink dress, tracing the white daisies stitched along the collar and hem. "I went shopping a few days ago to buy things for her."

Marianna snapped off the tag and dipped into the bag again. "I know she can't have them, but I needed to... I just couldn't let her birthday go by without celebrating it in some way."

A fabric doll came out next, tag snapped, toy placed to the side. "So I shopped." She cradled a little bathing suit—pink with yellow, blue and green fish. "I'm going to donate everything to charity."

"That's a really nice gesture." He should have thought to set up some kind of annual donation to a charity in Sophie's honor. It certainly wasn't too late, and he was learning that as much as he tried not to think about her, she still sprung into his mind at unexpected times. "What else did you pick out?"

"More clothes, of course. Smocked dresses and practical outfits too, for playing at the park. Bibs and shoes." She pulled out a traditional-looking teddy bear and hugged it to her chest. "Oh, and I bought her a stuffed animal from that store where you pick the pet and they stuff it for you."

"We had a discussion about the place once." He remembered Marianna going whimsical over the dream of having a birthday party for Sophie there one day.

Her eyes took on a faraway look as she stroked her thumbs along the plush fur. "Before they stuff it, you get a tiny red fabric heart to make a wish on then place inside the toy." A tear sparked in her eyes as her arms bit deeper into the stuffing. "So I prayed that she's happy and safe."

His chest felt heavy, his breath growing labored from the weight of trying to shore up the dam against images from the past. "You're killing me here, Marianna."

"I'm sorry." She turned slightly away and tucked the bear into a corner of the crib with heart twisting tenderness. "I shouldn't have rambled on so much. I know you prefer not to talk about her."

"No, it's not that," he finally admitted to himself and to her, even if the truth might push her away again. "It's killing me that I wasn't there for you how I should have been when she was taken away."

She angled back toward him, blinking fast. "You were grieving too, even if you didn't show it."

Marianna had been more magnanimous than he'd expected or probably even deserved. "Thank you for that."

"I know I should just be happy about this baby." She paused, her hands sliding over her stomach. "And I am, truly."

"Each child is just as important as the other." Hadn't his mother said much the same words at the hospital? He'd heard and comprehended in theory, but this time, the meaning sunk in with a deeper resonance.

"You understand." She extended a shaky hand, her eyes wary.

He hated that she had reason to doubt him when all he wanted was to make life easier for her. Sebastian clasped her fingers and tugged her forward until she sank into his lap. He gathered her closer, not sure how much time passed but at some point realizing he was staring at a framed photo on top of the armoire.

A picture of Marianna, Sophie and him at the baby's baptism.

Would he recognize his daughter if he passed her on the street? He liked to think so but couldn't be sure—babies changed so much so fast. Regardless, the time had come to accept that even if he saw her and knew her, she wouldn't remember them anymore.

"Sebastian?" Marianna's hands slid around him, linking behind his back. "You did hold me then, sometimes really late at night when I couldn't sleep."

"God, I don't even remember. That time is such a blur of…" He searched for the right word and could only come up with "…anger."

"You held me. You just wouldn't let me hold you." She tipped her face up to his, streaks on her face broadcasting the tears she'd cried silently. "But it's okay now. I know you miss her, and I know it's scary thinking about loving another child."

He grazed a kiss across her lips, keeping his hands firmly planted on the arms of the chair. Resisting the urge to pull out of her embrace because for some reason it made her happy to tear their hearts out this way.

And actually, simply kissing his wife had an appeal he hadn't fully appreciated until the privilege was taken away. His wife. While he hadn't doubted that he could win her back, he was damn glad things were moving along faster than he'd predicted when it came to bending her will.

The sooner he had his family together and taken care of, the better for all of them.

Sitting in Sebastian's car as he drove her to work, Marianna could barely believe all that had happened since they'd gotten into *her* car last night.

Kyle being shot down and recovering.

The car wreck and trip to the E.R.

Making love with Sebastian—and yes, she'd begun to hope they were beginning to make *love* with each other again.

The way he'd opened up to her in the nursery still took her breath away, filling her up again with hope. Sure, he hadn't spilled a wealth of words or emotionalism, but what he had shared felt like a fortune coming from her stalwart husband.

Ex-husband?

She wasn't quite ready to think in terms of marriage again so soon after their divorce, but for once, she wasn't completely crossing out the possibility. If he would just be patient with her, proving he'd changed his ways.

Sebastian chose a spot in the parking lot outside her office building, a quaint cottage on the beach. "I'll pick you up after work. I should finish with my court case on time. This judge has a reputation for keeping a tight stopwatch on proceedings."

She thought about asking him what sort of case, but work—his and hers—had been a sore spot between them. She didn't want to risk ruining their tenuous truce. "I appreciate your taking the evening off."

"I'm trying, Marianna."

"And that means a lot to me." She stared down at her clasped hands. "I noticed you spent some time at the computer last night."

He didn't miss a beat. "I couldn't sleep, not until I heard about Kyle."

That sounded reasonable, and she wouldn't have thought twice about the whole thing if it hadn't been for the past. Marianna reached across to cup his freshly shaved face, leaning to kiss him. He'd done so much of the pursuing lately that it was time to show him she was willing to meet him halfway. Inhaling the scent of his aftershave, tasting his mouthwash on his tongue, she savored the feel of his mouth against hers, familiar, yet with an edge of something new and exciting.

His hand slid to her stomach, palming just over where their baby nestled. She wanted to languish in the warm weight of his touch as much as she wanted to enjoy the sentimental gesture. But she couldn't shove aside the doubts that they were simply replaying the past. They'd gone through this dance when waiting to adopt, putting happy faces on the deeper troubles until the issues wounded, festered, left so many scars they'd eventually become numb.

She cut short the embrace, working to cover her unease. "We'll draw a crowd if we keep this up." She tapped his mouth. "But I promise we'll pick up where we left off. Tonight, I'll feed you while naked."

"It's a date." He winked his promise before stepping out of the car and around to her. He dropped a final quick kiss on her forehead, then climbed back behind the wheel.

Could she actually be watching his car pull away like the love-struck teen she'd once been? The twinge of uncertainty stirred inside her again, the fear he was playing along simply because of the baby as he'd done when Sophie entered their lives.

When would she believe he pursued her for herself? It all circled back around to trust taking time.

She backed toward the entrance, spinning along the door as she pushed inside. The lounge area buzzed lightly with piped in Muzak, their receptionist off to the left—and to the right, Ross waiting in her office door.

He shot her a wave. "Marianna, I need to speak with you for a minute."

"Sure," she answered, snagging her mail from the receptionist on her way to her office. "What do you need?"

Her boss closed the door after her, shutting them in the warm décor of her space, a place she'd decorated as a haven, complete with a soothing view of the Atlantic Ocean.

Ross followed her with lazy but even steps. "You can't actually be planning to take him back."

"You were watching us?" She tossed the mail and her purse onto her desk.

"Difficult to miss when you're right outside the building in broad daylight." He stroked his beard, his face tightening as if he was searching for words. "I just wanted to make sure you're all right."

Her skin prickled and not in a good way. This

wasn't playing out like a professional meeting. Could there have been something to Sebastian's suspicions? "While I appreciate your concern, this really isn't any of your business."

"I like to think we have more than a boss/ employee relationship. I consider you a friend."

Friend. She relaxed a little at the word. But not even for Ross could she hold back the tide of her emotions and the habit of speaking her mind. "As do I, but even friends need to be careful where they tread in offering relationship advice."

"See, here's the thing." He hitched his hands on his jeans loops, parting his jacket. "I did my level best to keep my emotions in check and my hands to myself while you were still with him. Married women are off-limits in my book."

Holy crap. Her feminine radar blared. "As they should be."

She crossed her arms over her chest, and if he knew anything about body language, he should read her back-off stance. Sebastian's sensors about Ross had been right. The man had feelings for her, even if he kept them to himself. How could she have missed picking up on that all these years they'd worked together?

Ross ambled a step nearer. "But you're not married now. I had planned to wait for you to get over the divorce, but I'm getting the sense that I may be short on time."

She swallowed down a hint of resentment for the

sake of professionalism, even as it angered her that he would tread into this terrain when she'd never given any indication she harbored those kinds of feelings for him. And he had seen her kissing Sebastian not five minutes ago.

"Please, don't say anything more." This conversation was spiraling out of control as fast as her spinning thoughts. She needed to make him understand he didn't have a chance with her—and she needed to do it before he messed up their working relationship forever.

"I will regret it for the rest of my life if I don't speak my mind." He crowded closer to her, backing her until her legs smacked an end table. "He doesn't appreciate you that way I do. Just give me a chance to show you how it could be between us." He pulled her to his chest.

She flattened her hands to his lapels to shove him away before he did something he would regret—or she said something she couldn't take back because it was getting harder and harder to put a cap on her mouth. "Ross, let's talk reasonably for a minute—"

The door clicked open, almost thudding against her as it swung wide. God, what would the receptionist think? Marianna shoved harder but Ross wouldn't budge.

"Hey, beautiful," Sebastian's voice echoed along with his footsteps against the carpet. "You forgot to eat breakf—"

She looked over Ross's shoulders as Sebastian came into sight. His gaze went from open to angry in a flash of dawning realization.

Marianna twisted free, searching for something to say other than the too cliché: *This isn't what it looks like.* She gripped Sebastian's arm, still so flustered at Ross's physical play for her she could barely comprehend this new turn of events. "Let's be reasonable adults—"

Sebastian shook his head without taking his gaze off the other man.

She felt so damn bad for Sebastian and how angry he must be over walking in on them, basically confirming for himself what he'd feared all along. "If you'll just step outside with me, we can sit in the car and talk."

"Talk?" Sebastian turned narrowed eyes toward her. "I don't think so, but I do think it would be a good idea if *you* step out of the room."

"Ross?" Again she tried to intercede. "Leave my office, please."

Her boss loped closer. "You're not going to be alone with him, not when he's in this kind of mood."

Sebastian eased his arm from her grip and turned his full attention to Ross. "Are you daring to insinuate I would ever hurt Marianna? You're the one hurting her by hitting on her in the workplace."

She stepped between the two men, certain neither of them would actually harm her. "Both of you, please take the testosterone level down a notch."

But neither of them was listening to her anymore.

Sebastian set her to the side with gentle hands at complete odds with the fury on his face. He pivoted on leather loafers to confront Ross. "I'm only going to say this once. Stay away from my wife."

Her boss didn't advance but he didn't back down either. "She's not yours anymore."

"Like hell. She's carrying my baby."

Marianna might have been tempted to laugh at the stunned expression on Ross's face—*if* she wasn't so steaming mad at the pigheaded father of her child for telling about the pregnancy. Even if he'd been right about Ross harboring feelings for her, she still stuck to her guns in believing Sebastian should know he could trust her.

How much better this would have played out if he'd simply put his arm around her and said they were working on their problems. Apparently Sebastian could only change so much at a time. She opened her mouth to demand Ross deliver an apology and explanations for stepping out of line.

Only to stop short as her ex-husband hauled back his fist and decked her soon to be ex-boss.

Sebastian might have been tempted to smile over how fast and hard Ross fell back onto the sofa.

Might have.

But rage steamed too hot and furious. The bastard wasn't wasting any time moving in on Marianna. Having all those jealous convictions confirmed only served to fuel Sebastian's anger.

He shook out his fist, angling toward Marianna, who must undoubtedly be shaken by what her boss had done. From the corner of his eye, he spotted a flurry of movement. Ross Ward surged up from the floor, tackling him at the waist. What the—?

Sebastian slammed back against the wall, rattling the Monet print by his head. Nose to nose with the object of too many marital fights, he couldn't hold his fury in check any longer.

In some distant part of his brain, he heard people gathering in the open doorway as Marianna shouted, "Stop!"

He stole a quick glance to make sure she was staying a safe distance away. Ward clipped him across the jaw.

Damn, that actually hurt. Sebastian threw all his muscle into sending the poaching jackass crashing back into the tapestry chair.

The fight visibly slid out of Ward as he sagged into the seat. "Baby?"

Marianna nodded, her lips tight with unmistakable frustration. "It's true. I'm two months along."

Frustration? If anyone deserved to be mad, he did. Ward had plastered his slimy hands all over

Marianna. Even thinking about seeing her so close to the other guy sent Sebastian seeing red. He kept an eye on Ward in case he decided to launch a surprise attack.

Gasping in the armchair, her boss worked his jaw. "I'm going to sue your ass for assault." Ward looked over at the three people standing in the doorway— the receptionist and two strangers who must be clients. "You're all witnesses to what happened here."

Sebastian stepped closer, staring the man down. "Go ahead and try it. I'll smack a countersuit against you so fast it'll fry that overly groomed beard off your face. Even a first-year law student could see your behavior constitutes sexual harassment in the workplace."

Marianna's mouth went tighter as she strode across the room to close the door on the now gaping onlookers. She pivoted back around, her hands behind her on the brass knob.

"Both of you, stop it. I don't *belong* to either one of you." She turned to her boss. "I intend to speak with you later, but not now. Will you please step out so I can talk to the father of my child?"

As Ross left the room, Sebastian blinked back his surprise at Marianna's words. Hearing her officially acknowledge their child for the first time sent a charge through him like nothing he'd felt since…since they brought Sophie home. And damn, that thought sideswiped him far harder than any punch from Ward. Except for once, Sebastian didn't want to close off that thought.

He willingly let a happy memory of his daughter flood his brain until Marianna slid into his line of sight, cutting short the moment.

"Sebastian, you were right about him having feelings for me. I'm sorry I didn't listen to you."

He hadn't expected that to come out of her pretty mouth. "Okay then. We're on the same page. Do you want me to get moving boxes or are there some around here that we can use to load up your office supplies?"

She patted his chest softly, unmistakably conciliatory. "You're steamrolling me again. If I decide to quit, I can pack up my own office."

"If?" His frustration shifted from Ward to Marianna. "What the hell are you talking about? Your boss just hit on you."

"You seem to be missing the most important point." She smoothed his tie, tightening the knot, which must have gone askew during the fight. "You had absolutely no reason to be jealous."

He grasped her wrists to stop her nervous motions. "The guy wants to have sex with you. That's reason enough."

"There are women out there who want to have sex with you. Should I tear their hair out? Of course not." She eased her hands from his grip, the six inches between them suddenly seeming a helluva lot wider. "I need for you to trust me, trust that I will make the right decision here. I'm not an unsure teenager anymore. I can take care of myself."

"You're turning this all around." Some lawyerly logic would serve him well right now, except logical was the last thing he felt around Marianna. "Listen, it's not as if we need the money. While I was on the computer last night, I came up with some ideas for investing in a trust fund for the baby. I can set up an account for you by the close of business today."

"Do not go there, Sebastian," she snapped, her chest rising and falling faster and faster with each breath. "Nothing's changed, has it? What makes you think we can just go back to the way things were?"

Her words seeped into his brain, and he wasn't liking the implication one bit. "So you're saying that's it. No trying, not even for the baby."

"I'm saying because of the baby we have to find a way to communicate without tearing each other apart." Marianna stood her ground even as her jaw trembled. "And if that means we can't be together anymore, then that's the way it has to be."

All her talk of making *love* had been just that. Talk.

"You're taking that job in Columbia, aren't you?"

"It's not about the job or the damn money." Anger crackled from her as she all but stamped her foot. "I don't care about your bank balance. This is about your trying to manipulate me into doing things your way. This is about you and me and the way you don't trust me to have handled what happened today."

"Did you ever think maybe you don't trust me?"

That stopped her short and he couldn't miss the hint of guilt that clouded her eyes. She didn't even deny what he'd said. She hadn't trusted him. He kept his hands jammed in his pockets, calling up all restraint. He wasn't the type to shout down any woman, much less a pregnant woman he loved.

Loved?

Hell yes, he loved her. He'd loved her since they were teenagers, and yet they still ended up in this same place time after time.

But that knowledge didn't stop him from pushing the issue. Fighting for this one last bit of understanding from her about a major cause of arguments in the past. "I was right about Ross Ward. All this time he's had feelings for you."

"Of course you're right." Tears welled and she scraped her wrist over her face. "You're always right and I'm just the emotional explosion waiting to happen. You never seemed to consider that I'm a big girl. I can handle a man being attracted to me and keep him at arm's distance."

"Yeah, you were doing real well with that when I came in here."

If he'd hoped to wound her—and hell, maybe

he had—he could see he'd done a damn good job of it. Her face paled. Her lips tightened into a hard, flat line.

"Get out, Sebastian." She turned her back to him, the set to her shoulders making it clear she was done talking, likely done with *them*. "Just leave."

Eleven

The door closed in her now-empty office with a finality that reverberated all the way to Marianna's toes. Even in the quiet aftermath with only the swoosh-swoosh of the grandfather clock to keep her company, the sounds of Sebastian's fight with her boss—the sounds of her fight with Sebastian—lingered.

How had things gone so wrong so fast? Her heart squeezed tight in her chest as she thought of the brief hope she'd felt earlier. How she'd actually thought because he spoke Sophie's name everything else might magically fall into place.

They'd taken a long time getting to this sad and

confusing place in their relationship. She'd been foolish to think that years of problems could be solved in the span of a few days. God, it hurt loving such a quietly immovable man.

Marianna sank onto the sofa, exhausted, and it wasn't even lunchtime yet. She considered going after Sebastian before he could pull out of the parking lot—for all of two swooshes of the pendulum. She didn't even know where to begin sorting through this.

The only fact she knew for sure? She needed to turn in her notice. What Sebastian had wanted from the start.

Had he let things get out of control with the fight, knowing that would leave her no choice but to resign? Could he be that manipulative? He'd tried to maneuver her about the money and stopping work altogether. In fact, from the moment Sebastian had heard she was pregnant, he'd launched in about her quitting her job—any job. She hated the creeping suspicions that he could be so calculating in getting his way.

She looked around her office and said her mental goodbyes to this corner of her life, which suddenly didn't feel all that important when she thought of everything else she could lose today. Sebastian. The possibility of a future with him.

Marianna shoved to her feet, resigned to getting past her meeting with Ross. She ignored the curious stares as she strode through the lobby and into the sleek blues and silvers of Ross's office.

Leaving the door very wide open.

He seemed to size her up as he finished a phone call and replaced the receiver into a cradle on his mahogany desk. From the dark rocks in the waterfall fountain sculpture along one wall to the stark, structural paintings over the couch, everything about his space underscored a quiet masculinity that had won him awards for his designs.

How much of her own success had trickled down from opportunities he'd given her out of a need to slide into her good graces? She would never know for sure, but it presented yet another reason she couldn't work here any longer. She deserved to realize her own strengths, to test how far she could go on her own merits.

Ross tipped back his chair with a creak, his jaw already purpling from the impact of Sebastian's fist. His gaze flicked from the lobby, then back to her. "What can I do for you, Marianna?"

Her heart drummed in her ears, adrenaline pumping through her veins, urging her on. "I appreciate the opportunities I've had here, and I've always respected your talent. But I can't work for you any longer."

He leaned forward with a long squeak of the chair. "Marianna, please take a seat so I can expl—"

Her sense of rightness about what she was doing forced her to interrupt.

"I won't be here long enough to sit." She stopped well shy of his desk, anger simmering anew at the way he'd backed her quite literally into a corner earlier. "I'm only here to tell you I'll be turning in my written two weeks' notice this afternoon."

He started to rise and she took another instinctive step toward the door. Ross sank into his seat, angling forward, his voice low. "I told you I never would have made a move on you as long as you were married, and I meant it. If you and he are getting together again, I won't be happy, but I won't interfere."

He seemed to be telling the truth, and in that moment she felt a twinge of sympathy for him. She understood well how painful it was to have feelings for someone only to be shut out. However she couldn't let that understanding affect her decision.

She bit back the urge to chew him out for causing such chaos in her life. For not listening when she'd told him to stop. None of which would help any of them. She needed a clean cut here, regardless of how things worked out with the father of her child.

"Sebastian has a problem with my working here, and I should have respected his feelings. He and I need to find a more level footing for the baby's sake."

"Does that mean you two *are* back together?"

Were they? She wasn't sure. How they would build a future with each other still seemed unclear to her. However, a sense of peace settled inside her as she stood here *calmly* fighting her own battle.

A sense that she was strong enough to stand on her own, to make hard decisions for her and for her child.

"I honestly don't know, Ross. But I do know I'm not available."

She turned away, her head high as she walked past the people in the lobby now trying too hard *not* to look at her. Marianna strode back toward her office to call a cab and retrieve her purse, reveling in her own strength and the knowledge that she would be okay. People respected her and her work, and just because Ross had been a jerk to her wouldn't change that.

Snatching the phone up, she turned as she punched in the stored number she used to set up rides for clients. Mid-dial, she noticed a flash of white across the room. A small white bag. Had it been there when she arrived?

Lowering the phone and thumbing the off button, she plucked up the sack, the logo solving the mystery. The bag had come from the store where Sebastian bought the flavored peanut butters. Hadn't he said something about her missing breakfast when he arrived? He must have packed the snack for her while she rushed to get ready for work.

Their day could have turned out so differently if she'd been alone in her office. But she also knew they would have only been delaying the inevitable. At some point, this showdown would have erupted.

She opened the fold and looked inside to find…a

cinnamon crunch bagel with a little plastic container of spiced peanut butter. Tucked in the bottom of the bag was one of Sebastian's business cards with a scrawl on the back.

"Love, S," she whispered rubbing her thumb along the simple note.

Love. It felt like forever since he'd used that word. Was he trying to apologize for not saying it last night? Of course she hadn't told him either, only hinting at the subject.

The bag seemed to grow heavier in her hand, its significance weighing on her conscience. She thought of other thoughtful gestures he'd made in the past that she'd chalked up to calculation. What if maybe, just maybe, those could have been attributed to affection rather than manipulation?

She turned the possibility over in her mind. He'd said often that being a lawyer led him to deal with deceitful people on a regular basis. That could certainly wear at a person's ability to trust in words. Actions would count more for him.

It stood to reason her reserved ex would have tried to *show* the love he couldn't voice.

She wasn't sure how she would persuade Sebastian to open up or how they would wade through the mess they'd made of their love for each other. But she wasn't going to quit trying if there was a chance he still wanted to save what they had together. Marianna stuffed the tiny sack into her purse and hooked the leather handbag over her shoulder.

Now she just needed to find which courtroom he was in—and figure out a way to make her own case to Sebastian in a way that would win over one of the best litigators in South Carolina.

Marianna sat in the back row of the courtroom, energized by her new determination even more than by the bagel she'd devoured on the way over.

Sebastian rose from his seat behind the table, buttoning his suit coat. A charcoal gray suit she'd chosen for him a week before they'd split. She'd never had the chance to see him wear it before today. The lightweight summer fabric hugged his broad shoulders even more perfectly than she'd expected. His close-trimmed hair only just kissed the top of his collar, calling to mind the silky texture.

He didn't appear to notice her, not even missing a beat in questioning the witness. Something to do with defending a mother and her son against an abusive father. Looking at his clients, it was obvious Sebastian had taken this case pro bono, and seeing the flame of hope in that young mother's eyes, Marianna admired him for the choice he'd made.

Sebastian went after the witness—the hulking father with fists clenched on his thighs—keeping a calm drive and focus that subtly shifted to a more heated push for the truth. Again and again he challenged the witness with questions that probed free unwitting admissions, each nugget strengthening his case.

She got lost in watching Sebastian at his fiery litigator best, this man she didn't see at home. Even knowing he was reputed to be tops at his job hadn't prepared her for the full impact of seeing him in action. He poured all that emotional energy into fighting for a child who couldn't defend himself.

Marianna inched to the edge of her seat, the deep power of Sebastian's voice filling the courtroom. In a flash of inspiration, she realized he hadn't been avoiding his feelings at all. He was pouring his frustrations over losing Sophie into defending this child. And just as surely she knew he delivered the same intensity for all his clients. He'd become the kind of lawyer he'd always said he wanted to be back in the days when they'd dreamed.

Maybe as his plan played out, he hadn't expected to use up most of his best arguing here. Was it any wonder he wanted peace at home?

The new understanding swelled inside her, along with a sense of how she could fit into his life in an unexpected way. God, she would enjoy playing devil's advocate for a case. Or perhaps showing up in the courtroom now and then, being a part of *his* world instead of always waiting for him to be a part of hers.

She hadn't been wrong in thinking it would take

time to trust each other again. But now, seeing this dazzling glimpse of the man she'd fallen for in the first place, she was willing to do whatever it took, for as long as it took.

Sebastian knew the minute Marianna walked into the courtroom. Even with his back turned, he got that unmistakable sensation telling him she was near. He hadn't missed a beat in his case, but he'd sure been counting down the minutes until they broke for lunch.

His watch showed him noon just as the prompt judge rapped her gavel for a recess. Sebastian took a moment to reassure his client before finally shifting his full attention to the back of the courtroom.

He charged down the aisle, Marianna waiting there in the last row, not moving toward him or even standing. Was she here to finish venting her anger at him? He'd lost his cool with Ward, but even with his fist throbbing and Marianna's anger in his ears, he wasn't sure he would do anything differently. The way he saw it, he'd been protecting his wife and child.

He paused midstep, realizing that just because he was right about Ward didn't mean Marianna's day had sucked any less. Sebastian had known all along that the guy had been gunning for her, but she'd been caught off guard, disillusioned and manhandled to boot. And while he'd felt justified in firing off his anger on her employer, maybe he could have offered her some kind of…comfort.

Guilt nipped at his heels. He could almost see his mother shaking a well-manicured finger at him for not making time to take better care of Marianna. Of his family.

Then Marianna smiled. And he knew, deserved or not, he'd been given a reprieve, one he damn well intended to use to the fullest.

She crooked her finger for him to lean toward her. "Sebastian," she whispered, "find a broom closet or empty conference room pronto, please."

He didn't need to be told twice. Even if he'd found some aspects of marriage to a feisty female a challenge, he's always savored this side of her. Marianna might never back down from a fight, but then again, she never held back when she wanted *this*.

Sebastian clasped her elbow and guided her toward the same conference room where he'd carried her just a few short days ago when she'd passed out after their divorce decree. Once inside the room, *she* flattened *him* to the door, arching up to kiss him before he could so much as say hello. Of course who was he to argue with a greeting that beat the hell out of any words?

He met and answered the bold sweeps of her tongue against his, only the lack of a lock keeping him from lowering her to the sofa. God, this woman had been knocking him on his butt for nine years and counting. No problems between them had ever changed that.

She gasped against his mouth. "I gave my two weeks' notice right after you left."

And he'd thought her kisses knocked him flat.

"Because of what I did?" He stared down at her, trying to gauge every nuance of her mood.

"I should have listened to your concerns about Ross earlier." Her fingers toyed with the hair along the back of his neck. "But I quit because it was the right thing to do. He was out of line."

"What do you plan to do now?"

Tension pinched lines along the corners of her eyes, stealing some of the spark. "I hope this isn't a lead-in to you offering to fill my bank account."

He stayed silent, weighing the best answer. He'd been so focused on winning, somewhere along the line he'd forgotten about the power of compromise. The best lawyers realized some instances called for bargaining. She'd made a major concession in giving notice to Ward. Time to reciprocate. Keeping her in his life was too important to screw up again.

"How about I fill your refrigerator with things to tempt your palate instead?"

"Thank you." Her smile provided a bigger payoff than he could have predicted.

Sebastian cupped her face. "I'm sorry I made a scene at your office."

He'd always respected her work, admiring the way she brought beauty to everything she touched.

He hadn't intended to mess any of that up for her. With a cooler temper now, he sincerely hoped he hadn't compromised her ability to take her professional skills wherever she chose.

She stilled against him, her eyes wide and unblinking so long he started to worry about her.

"Marianna? Is something wrong?"

She shook her head slowly. "Do you realize that's the first time you've ever apologized to me?"

What was she talking about? "That can't be right. I've worked like crazy to get back into your good graces more times than I can count."

"I do see better now how you've tried over the years. But I have to confess, counselor, that sometimes it's still helpful to hear the words."

"Makes sense, I imagine. You are a woman who likes a good, long discussion."

Then it hit him. She needed the words when it came to more than apologies. She wanted more than signs of his love.

She had to hear the words.

"I love you, Marianna." He worked with speeches all day long. How could he have missed the boat so thoroughly when it counted the most? "Not just because you're the mother of my children—Sophie and this baby and any others we may have or adopt. But because you fire me up, challenge me to be more, and God knows I have a reputation around the courthouse for enjoying a good challenge."

Since he was also a man of action, he cemented his declaration with another kiss. Marianna leaned into him, her soft curves melding against him. The need to make love, seal their commitment, burned inside him, something he intended to follow up on the minute he got her home tonight.

Marianna took two steps back, keeping their fingers linked until the very…last…second. Hands on her waist, she jutted one hip forward, her leg extended to show off just how hot she made pink designer pumps look. His body tightened with the familiar jolt of desire.

With a defiant toss of her tangled curls, she met his gaze dead-on, with complete honesty and conviction. "I love you, Sebastian Landis. I love your sexy body when it caresses mine. I love your brilliant mind when it challenges mine. I love your peanut buttery thoughtful soul when it touches mine. I love you, unconditionally, forever."

Sebastian felt the waves of her healing love wash over him, chasing away the last whispers of that old nightmare. "Where do you see us going from here?"

She nibbled her lip, and he hated that he'd made her hesitant in voicing what she wanted. He looped his arms low around her waist and brought her close again.

Marianna smoothed the lapels of his suit, her hands tempting even through layers of clothes. "I would like to take time to get to rediscover each other."

Rather than hearing criticism because somehow he'd come up short in giving her enough, he heard her desire for both of them to have more. "Ah, you want to date."

"We did sort of skip over that when we met."

Theirs had been a quick trip to the altar. Had she been carrying around insecurities from that all these years? Something he definitely needed to fix, because he knew, without question, he would have walked this fascinating woman down the aisle, baby or no baby.

He skimmed his knuckles down her cheek. "How about we get a start on that the minute the judge wraps up for the day. No working late for me tonight. I have a special lady to take out who happens to enjoy fine dining."

Her brown eyes glinted with wicked promise. "Lucky for you, I just bought a new pair of shoes to model on our first date."

Epilogue

8 1/2 months later:

Marianna always welcomed the chance to buy a new pair of shoes. And today's event provided the most exciting reason for a shopping spree yet.

Searching for Sebastian among the small crowd at the reception, she wove by the guests milling around the Landis compound pool. Rose petals floated along the surface, the afternoon sunlight sparking prisms off the water while family and a few close friends finished an after-lunch cocktail.

As she walked along the glazed brick, her French pedicure peeked from her cream-colored open-toed heels, a Chanel purchase that had paid off more than once during the day with heated looks from Sebastian. Her off-white silk dress wrapped around her new curves, caressing just below her knees with each swishing step.

The months with Sebastian hadn't always been easy, but the time spent getting to know each other again had proved the *best* investment either of them had ever made. Without question, Sebastian would always be a powerfully driven man, but she no longer doubted her ability to stand up to him and win her point on occasion. She'd learned to lean a bit more on logic, and he'd learned to listen to his heart when it counted.

Today's gathering, however, wasn't about them. It was all about someone else.

This afternoon, they celebrated the baptism of Edward Sebastian Landis—all healthy seven pounds, eleven ounces of him at birth, heavier now, of course with little Edward hitting his six-week birthday.

Her feet slowed as she paused for a glance across the pool to check on her son—she couldn't look at his precious face often enough—and found Edward still sleeping soundly in his grandmother's arms. Ginger held court at a poolside table, showing off her new grandchild from under the shade of the protective umbrella. His traditional, long baptismal gown would go on display next to Sophie's at the end of the day.

A warm palm flattened to Marianna's waist, pulling her back to the moment. She didn't even have to look over her shoulder. She knew that touch intimately well.

Sebastian slid his arm around to lean her back against his chest. "You and Mom sure do know how to throw a great party."

His breath caressed her ear, the low rumble of his voice sending a shiver of excitement tingling along her skin as she remembered just how well and often they'd come together over the past months. They'd stayed away from the subject of marriage though. More than once she'd appreciated his patience in giving her the time she needed to lay her fears to rest by working out some of their problems before saying *I do* again.

She tipped her head to look up into his face, the angular lines that could be so forbidding in court eased by unmistakable happiness. "I have to commend you for giving feedback on the menu for the first time since I've known you."

"Hmmm…I didn't realize that providing you with a list of candies from the peanut butter store constituted feedback."

"I thought it was a sweet and sentimental gesture."

"Sweet? Shhh…" He turned and tugged her away from the crowd and under the privacy of a rose-covered wooden trellis. "Good God, Marianna, don't let my brothers hear that. They'll give me hell on the golf course."

Something he did more often now—golfing and hanging out with his family. He even vowed the extra downtime made him more effective at work.

She teased her pointer finger along his mouth, the ocean breeze wafting the sweet smell from roses clinging to the arbor overhead. "Your secret is safe with me."

They'd both made adjustments in their professional lives. Her decision to stop working with Ross had actually unchained her creativity beyond anything she would have ever dreamed. After considering a number of job offers, she'd decided to branch out on her own. She'd spent the past few months building an online business for interior decorating. People sent photos of their homes, and she offered simple improvement plans for a wide range of budgets—including using furniture already in place as well as listing items for purchase in their area and over the Internet.

She'd also been inspired by how Sebastian allowed his financial security to free up time to represent clients who couldn't otherwise afford even an hour of his billable rate. Her booming new business also took on special interest homes on a sliding scale according to client need. Just last week, she'd finished plans to revamp a house for a family financially stretched from the birth of quadruplets.

She'd found so much fulfillment organizing the space to give those children as much room and privacy as possible, while ensuring the parents had some special retreat spots, too. She'd come to realize how important it was to nurture your love relationship and not take it for granted for even a moment.

Sebastian plucked a rose from the trellis and grazed it along her cheek before tucking it behind her ear. "I've been thinking that perhaps we can tap Mom to throw another party for us."

Without question, the Landises had much to rejoice about lately. Matthew had won his senatorial seat; he and Ashley now married and settled into traveling between their D.C. residence and South Carolina home. His mother was a dynamo in her Secretary of State position. She and the General made the news on a regular basis as one of the U.S.'s most powerful political couples.

"What kind of party?" Marianna smoothed his lapels, thinking of how they almost hadn't managed to get dressed in time this morning with the mattress tempting them both after six weeks of abstinence.

"An engagement party." He pulled his hand from his pocket, along with a ring box.

"The timing is perfect." She reveled in the hard-earned joy of this union, so much different from the first rushed proposal based on circumstance and need.

They'd had chance after chance to walk away from each other, but this marriage would be based on the knowledge that their love was too great to be denied. Too special ever to be taken for granted again.

He hauled her to his chest, his heart picking up speed against her ear, broadcasting how important this was to him in spite of his seeming calm. She breathed in the familiar scent of his aftershave mixed with a hint of Edward's baby powder freshness.

"Marianna, will you marry me—again?" He creaked open the box to reveal a pear-shaped diamond alongside a diamond-studded band. "It's a new ring, but with an anniversary band."

She traced along the line of gems, counting. "This would have been our tenth year." They'd come a long way from two near strangers marrying as teens. She let tears flow that had nothing to do with postnatal hormones and everything to do with pure, undiluted happiness. "I like the blending of the old and new together. It's perfect. Yes, I will marry you, Sebastian Landis."

He thumbed her cheeks dry. Then slid the engagement diamond onto her finger where it settled with a perfect rightness, waiting for the band to be placed beside on their wedding day.

Sebastian closed his hand around hers in a grip as strong and steady as the man. "Just so we're clear. We're not getting married because you were pregnant, although I certainly wouldn't complain if you got pregnant again someday."

Marianna thought of the new photo on their mantel, a picture of Sophie that her birth mother had sent through their case worker. There wouldn't be any contact, and at this point Marianna feared confusing her anyway. She would always ache to hold her, would miss her every day, but she'd found a peace in seeing the happiness in Sophie's eyes—the eyes of a little girl well-loved.

She had to ask, "And if we never have another child?"

He was an amazing father, so patient in walking the floor at midnight with Edward cradled in his strong arms.

Sebastian brushed a windswept lock of her hair behind her ear with the flower. "I'm okay with that, too. I want *you* in my life."

"What a wonderful coincidence." The bloom's sweet scent mingled with the ocean breeze carrying the voices of the happy guests. "That's exactly where I want to be."

He hooked an arm around her shoulders, slipping a teasing finger just under the strap of her dress. "How about we retrieve our son from his grandmother and head home to Buddy and Holly?"

"We do have a lot to celebrate." She slid her hand under his suit jacket, his hard, lean body tempting her to explore him without the barrier of clothing. A pleasure she knew she would enjoy for the rest of their lives together. "In fact, I was thinking an intimate celebration is definitely in order."

His eyes glinted with the promise of deep and leisurely kisses to come once they were completely alone. "So who gets to feed whom naked this time?"

"That all depends on who gets their clothes off first."

* * * * *

THE LANDIS BROTHERS *series will continue. But don't miss Catherine Mann's next release, PROPOSITIONED INTO A FOREIGN AFFAIR, coming in May 2009 from Silhouette Desire.*

Turn the page for a sneak preview of
AFTERSHOCK, *a new anthology
featuring* New York Times *bestselling author
Sharon Sala.*

Available October 2008.

n●cturne™

*Dramatic and sensual tales
of paranormal romance.*

Chapter 1

October
New York City

Nicole Masters was sitting cross-legged on her sofa while a cold autumn rain peppered the windows of her fourth-floor apartment. She was poking at the ice cream in her bowl and trying not to be in a mood.

Six weeks ago, a simple trip to her neighborhood pharmacy had turned into a nightmare. She'd walked into the middle of a robbery. She never even saw the man who shot her in the head and left her for dead. She'd survived, but some of her senses had not. She was dealing with short-term memory loss and a tendency to stagger. Even though she'd been told the problems were most likely temporary, she waged a daily battle with depression.

Her parents had been killed in a car wreck when she was twenty-one. And except for a few friends—and most recently her boyfriend, Dominic Tucci, who lived in the apartment right above hers, she was alone. Her doctor kept reminding her that she should be grateful to be alive, and on one level she knew he was right. But he wasn't living in her shoes.

If she'd been anywhere else but at that pharmacy when the robbery happened, she wouldn't have died twice on the way to the hospital. Instead of being grateful that she'd survived, she couldn't stop thinking of what she'd lost.

But that wasn't the end of her troubles. On top of everything else, something strange was happening inside her head. She'd begun to hear odd things: sounds, not voices—at least, she didn't think it was voices. It was more like the distant noise of rapids—a rush of wind and water inside her head that, when it came, blocked out everything around her. It didn't happen often, but when it did, it was frightening, and it was driving her crazy.

The blank moments, which is what she called them, even had a rhythm. First there came that sound, then a cold sweat, then panic with no reason.

Part of her feared it was the beginning of an emotional breakdown. And part of her feared it wasn't—that it was going to turn out to be a permanent souvenir of her resurrection.

Frustrated with herself and the situation as it stood, she upped the sound on the TV remote. But instead of *Wheel of Fortune,* an announcer broke in with a special bulletin.

"This just in. Police are on the scene of a kidnapping that occurred only hours ago at The Dakota. Molly Dane, the six-year-old daughter of one of Hollywood's blockbuster stars, Lyla Dane, was taken by force from the family apartment. At this time they have yet to receive a ransom demand. The housekeeper was seriously injured during the abduction, and is, at the present time, in surgery. Police are hoping to be able to talk to her once she regains consciousness. In the meantime, we are going now to a press conference with Lyla Dane."

Horrified, Nicole stilled as the cameras went live to where the actress was speaking before a bank of microphones. The shock and terror in Lyla Dane's voice were physically painful to watch. But even though Nicole kept upping the volume, the sound continued to fade.

Just when she was beginning to think something was wrong with her set, the broadcast suddenly switched from the Dane press conference to what appeared to be footage of the kidnapping, beginning with footage from inside the apartment.

When the front door suddenly flew back against the wall and four men rushed in, Nicole gasped. Horrified, she quickly realized that this must have been caught on a security camera inside the Dane apartment.

As Nicole continued to watch, a small Asian woman, who she guessed was the maid, rushed forward in an effort to keep them out. When one of the men hit her in the face with his gun, Nicole moaned. The violence was too reminiscent of what she'd lived through. Sick to her stomach, she fisted her hands against her belly, wishing it was over, but unable to tear her gaze away.

When the maid dropped to the carpet, the same man followed with a vicious kick to the little woman's midsection that lifted her off the floor.

"Oh, my God," Nicole said. When blood began to pool beneath the maid's head, she started to cry.

As the tape played on, the four men split up in different directions. The camera caught one running down a long marble hallway, then disappearing into a room. Moments later he reappeared, carrying a little girl, who Nicole assumed was Molly Dane. The child was wearing a pair of red pants and a white turtleneck sweater, and her hair was partially blocking her abductor's face as he carried her down the hall. She was kicking and screaming in his arms, and when he slapped her, it elicited an agonized scream that brought the other three running. Nicole watched in horror as one of them ran up and put his hand over Molly's face. Seconds later, she went limp.

One moment they were in the foyer, then they were gone.

Nicole jumped to her feet, then staggered drunkenly. The bowl of ice cream she'd absentmindedly placed in her lap shattered at her feet, splattering glass and melting ice cream everywhere.

The picture on the screen abruptly switched from the kidnapping to what Nicole assumed was a rerun of Lyla Dane's plea for her daughter's safe return, but she was numb.

Before she could think what to do next, the doorbell rang. Startled by the unexpected sound, she shakily swiped at the tears and took a step forward. She didn't feel the glass shards piercing her feet until she took the second step. At that point, sharp pains shot through her foot. She gasped, then looked down in confusion. Her legs looked as if she'd been running through mud, and she was standing in broken glass and ice cream, while a thin ribbon of blood seeped out from beneath her toes.

"Oh, no," Nicole mumbled, then stifled a second moan of pain.

The doorbell rang again. She shivered, then clutched her head in confusion.

"Just a minute!" she yelled, then tried to sidestep the rest of the debris as she hobbled to the door.

When she looked through the peephole in the door, she didn't know whether to be relieved or regretful.

It was Dominic, and as usual, she was a mess.

Nicole smiled a little self-consciously as she opened the door to let him in. "I just don't know what's happening to me. I think I'm losing my mind."

"Hey, don't talk about my woman like that."

Nicole rode the surge of delight his words brought. "So I'm still your woman?"

Dominic lowered his head.

Their lips met.

The kiss proceeded.

Slowly.

Thoroughly.

* * * * *

Be sure to look for the
AFTERSHOCK *anthology next month,*
as well as other exciting paranormal stories
from Silhouette Nocturne.
Available in October wherever books are sold.

Silhouette

nocturne™

NEW YORK TIMES BESTSELLING AUTHOR

SHARON SALA

JANIS REAMES HUDSON
DEBRA COWAN

AFTERSHOCK

Three women are brought to the brink of death...
only to discover the aftershock of their trauma has
left them with unexpected and unwelcome gifts of
paranormal powers. Now each woman must learn to
accept her newfound abilities while fighting for life,
love and second chances....

Available October wherever books are sold.

www.eHarlequin.com
www.paranormalromanceblog.wordpress.com   SN61796

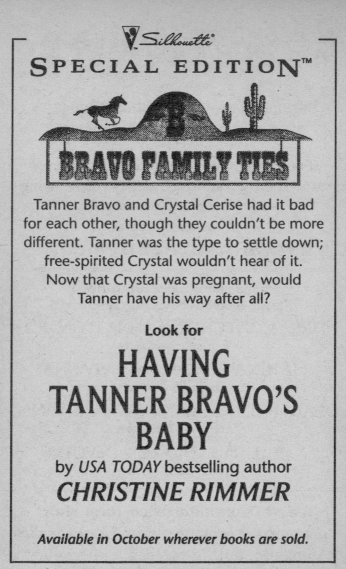

SPECIAL EDITION™

BRAVO FAMILY TIES

Tanner Bravo and Crystal Cerise had it bad
for each other, though they couldn't be more
different. Tanner was the type to settle down;
free-spirited Crystal wouldn't hear of it.
Now that Crystal was pregnant, would
Tanner have his way after all?

Look for

HAVING TANNER BRAVO'S BABY

by *USA TODAY* bestselling author
CHRISTINE RIMMER

Available in October wherever books are sold.

REQUEST YOUR FREE BOOKS!

2 FREE NOVELS
PLUS 2
FREE GIFTS!

Silhouette®

Desire®

Passionate, Powerful, Provocative!

YES! Please send me 2 FREE Silhouette Desire® novels and my 2 FREE gifts (gifts are worth about $10). After receiving them, if I don't wish to receive any more books, I can return the shipping statement marked "cancel". If I don't cancel, I will receive 6 brand-new novels every month and be billed just $4.05 per book in the U.S. or $4.74 per book in Canada, plus 25¢ shipping and handling per book and applicable taxes, if any*. That's a savings of almost 15% off the cover price! I understand that accepting the 2 free books and gifts places me under no obligation to buy anything. I can always return a shipment and cancel at any time. Even if I never buy another book, the two free books and gifts are mine to keep forever.

225 SDN ERVX 326 SDN ERVM

Name	(PLEASE PRINT)	
Address		Apt. #
City	State/Prov.	Zip/Postal Code

Signature (if under 18, a parent or guardian must sign)

Mail to the Silhouette Reader Service:

IN U.S.A.: P.O. Box 1867, Buffalo, NY 14240-1867
IN CANADA: P.O. Box 609, Fort Erie, Ontario L2A 5X3

Not valid to current subscribers of Silhouette Desire books.

Want to try two free books from another line?
Call 1-800-873-8635 or visit www.morefreebooks.com.

* Terms and prices subject to change without notice. N.Y. residents add applicable sales tax. Canadian residents will be charged applicable provincial taxes and GST. Offer not valid in Quebec. This offer is limited to one order per household. All orders subject to approval. Credit or debit balances in a customer's account(s) may be offset by any other outstanding balance owed by or to the customer. Please allow 4 to 6 weeks for delivery. Offer available while quantities last.

Your Privacy: Silhouette Books is committed to protecting your privacy. Our Privacy Policy is available online at www.eHarlequin.com or upon request from the Reader Service. From time to time we make our lists of customers available to reputable third parties who may have a product or service of interest to you. If you would prefer we not share your name and address, please check here. ☐

SDES08R